TRAPHOUSE KING

Lock Down Publications and Ca$h
Presents
TRAPHOUSE KING
A Novel by *Hood Rich*

Lock Down Publications

P.O. Box 870494
Mesquite, Tx 75187

Visit our website @
www.lockdownpublications.com

Lock Down Publications
Like our page on Facebook: Lock Down Publications
@
www.facebook.com/lockdownpublications.ldp
Cover design and layout by: **Dynasty Cover Me**
Book interior design by: **Shawn Walker**
Edited by: **Sunny Giovanni**

Stay Connected with Us!

Text **LOCKDOWN** to 22828 to stay up-to-date with new releases, sneak peaks, contests and more…
Thank you.

Submission Guideline

Submit the first three chapters of your completed manuscript to ldpsubmissions@gmail.com, subject line: Your book's title. The manuscript must be in a .doc file and sent as an attachment. Document should be in Times New Roman, double spaced and in size 12 font. Also, provide your synopsis and full contact information. If sending multiple submissions, they must each be in a separate email.

Have a story but no way to send it electronically? You can still submit to LDP/Ca$h Presents. Send in the first three chapters, written or typed, of your completed manuscript to:

LDP: Submissions Dept
Po Box 870494
Mesquite, Tx 75187

DO NOT send original manuscript. Must be a duplicate.

Provide your synopsis and a cover letter containing your full contact information.

Thanks for considering LDP and Ca$h Presents.

Acknowledgements

I'd like to take the time to thank my homie, Cash. Thank you for providing me a platform to showcase my talents and skills. It means a lot. I'd also want to give a shout out to our C.O.O Shawn Walker. You are amazing, Queen. Thank you for always going so hard for Lock Down. We appreciate you, Queen.

Dedications

This book is dedicated to my lil' one. Everything Daddy do, he does it with you in mind. I love you with all that I am. Never forget that.

HOOD RICH

Chapter 1

My mother fell before my feet, looking up at me with eyes wide open. Tears slid down her cheeks as she wrapped her arms around herself and rocked back and forth, sobbing louder and louder. The black plastic garbage that we'd used to plug the hole in the broken window rattled continuously as the wind and rain blew harshly through the night's air. All around her on the floor were cockroaches the size of beetles, along with trash. It looked like she'd went more than a week once again without cleaning the house. It smelled like something was spoiled, and it was so cold that I could see my breath as I looked down on her with anger and a slight case of sympathy. After all, this was the woman that had given birth to me.

She pulled on my pants legs, nearly pulling my pants down altogether and her tears mixed with mascara staining her beautiful face. "Baby, please, give me a hit. I'm begging you. Mama so sick right now. It feels like my insides are being twisted. I can't take it. I need you." She whimpered, making her way to her feet, shaking as if she were freezing cold.

I looked down into her beautiful face and shook my head. "Mama, when you gon' let me put you in rehab? I'm tired of seeing you fighting this same struggle. Please let me take care of you." I begged, wiping her tears away.

She shook her head, and bit into her lower lip nervously. "Un-un, baby. Not right now. I'm not ready to go right now. I'm not strong enough. All I need is for you to give me a hit, baby. Just one hit and I promise I'll pay you back. You know I'm good for it. Has mommy ever lied to you?" She asked with a line of snot trailing out of her nose. She sniffed as hard as she could, drawing it back up.

I shook my head once again not knowing what to say to my mother, because the truth of the matter was that she'd been lying to me ever since I could remember. But I didn't feel there was any reason to kick her while she was down. "N'all, ma." I took a deep breath as my sixteen-year-old sister Keyonna came out of the back room with a blanket wrapped around her shoulders.

"Dang, mama, why you ain't tell me that Rich was here?" She asked, walking over to me and wrapping her arms around my waist. "How long you been here, Rich?" She asked, looking up at me with her hazel eyes. She was light skinned like myself, and on the right side of her upper lip was a little mole. I thought it made her look so beautiful. Besides my mother, my little sister Keyonna was my everything.

My mother grabbed Keyonna's arm aggressively and pulled her away from me. "Girl, can't you see that I was in here talking to him about something important?" She hollered with spit flying into my little sister's face.

Keyonna wiped her face, frowned and took a step back, looking our mother over with anger. "Dang, mama. I ain't seen my brother in a few days. I just wanted to give him a hug. It's not that serious." She rolled her eyes.

My mother took a step forward and reached out for Keyonna's neck with both of her small hands. "I done told this bitch about rolling her eyes at me. I'mma kill this heffa!" She screamed, then rushed Keyonna at full speed.

My sister backed all the way up until her back hit the wall, then she held her hands up defensively to block my mother from obtaining her throat. "Rich, get her away from me, please. I ain't trying to have her black my eye again!" Keyonna hollered trying her best to fight her off without actually fighting her.

I walked behind my mother and picked her up into the air, while she kicked her legs wildly, causing her house shoes to fly into the walls. Her arms swung at the air.

She seemed as if she was losing her mind. "I'm tired of that lil' bitch. Both of them. I want them hoes out of my house, Rich. I can't take this shit no more!" She screamed, referring to Keyonna and our other sister Kesha. This night, she wasn't home because she'd spent a night at my Aunt Leah's house.

I placed my mother on her feet and blocked her from getting out of the living room that had no furniture. Outside there was a loud roaring in the sky from the thunder, and the rain was coming down so hard that it sounded like rice was being poured out on to the concrete. Lightning flashed across the sky, illuminating the living room.

Keyonna blinked tears. "You know what? I don't wanna stay here no more either. I'm tired of all these men running in and out, and I'm tired of being your punching bag. I don't care if I gotta sleep on the street. I will, Rich. I'm so serious." She cried before running through the dining room and into the back of the house.

This seemed to infuriate my mother. She started to swing her arms wildly once again with her eyes closed. "Let me go so I can kill that bitch, Rich. That lil' girl so disrespectful. She don't appreciate shit!" She pulled on my polo shirt and ripped the collar.

I continued to block the doorway. "Look, mama, just chill. I'll take care of her and you, too. Here," I reached into my pocket of my Marc Jacobs leather jacket and pulled out the Ziploc bag full of aluminum foiled wrapped $10 heroin hits. I gave her three of them as much as it crushed my soul to do so. I figured it was the only way that she

11

would calm down and allow for me to get my sister out of the house without her trying to kill her for real.

You see, my mother had a temper that was so bad, that whenever she got mad she tended to black out. By the time she came to, she'd caused so much chaos that things were almost always ten times worst. So, I tried to avoid that from happening. I loved my sisters, and I wasn't cool with nobody putting their hands on them, and that included my mother. The comment Keyonna had made about so many men running in and out of the house I was going to explore as soon as I got her away from our mother.

My mother took the dope, took five paces away from me and fell to her butt, sitting Indian style. She pulled the sleeve of her sweater upward and started to smack the deteriorating vein at the top of her inner right arm, just below her bicep. Then in one quick motion she jumped up and came back into the living room with her works that consisted of a syringe, a spoon, a lighter, a rug, and a small bottle of water. I stood there with a tight throat as I watched her prepare the dope that I had given her. I was feeling like the worst son in the world but knowing that I really didn't have a choice. It made me sick to my stomach, and it took all the will power I had inside of me to not shed a tear, especially as I watched the needle go into her vein, before she pushed the feeder down, injecting the poison deep into her system.

As it began to flow, she closed her eyes and licked her lips. Smiling, two dimples appearing on each cheek. "Umm-hmm. That's what I'm talking about right there." She ran her tongue across her dry lips and squeezed her thighs together, before opening her eyes and looking me over in a daze. "You always take care of your mama, Rich.

It's the one thing I can say about you." She uttered through glossy eyes.

I inhaled loudly and exhaled, shaking my head, feeling like a straight chump. What type of nigga fed his mother drugs to keep her from wilding out? I felt like a loser on so many levels.

My mother reached forward and grabbed another package of heroin, opening it, and going through the same process as Keyonna came out of the back room with a book bag on her shoulder.

"I'm out of here, Rich. I can't take this crap no more." She stopped at the door and took her coat from the rack. Tears fell down her face as she zipped it up and pulled up the hood.

I frowned and stood in front of the door. "Look, Keyonna, I ain't about to let you go nowhere without me making sure you're straight. Just chill for a minute, and I'mma drop you off at Leah's crib until we can figure something else out. It's just so much going on that I can't think straight right now, but just chill out. Let me make sure mama straight, then we'll get you squared away. A'ight? Here, take my car keys and get in my whip. I'll be down in a minute." I handed her my keys and watched as she opened the door to the house.

She tightened her hood on her head and ran into the rain with her book bag on her shoulder.

I closed the door back just as lightning flashed across the sky. Thunder roared overhead. I turned to look down at my mother as she pushed the dropper downward on the syringe, sending the third hit of heroin into her body. The third hit that I had given her. "Mama, you need to take it easy with that stuff," I said feeling sick to my stomach. I wished that I could have taken her away from that drug, but ever since my father had gotten her addicted when I was only three years old, heroin had been an escape for her.

She looked up at me and attempted a smile, then her eyes got bucked, and she dropped the syringe that she'd been holding. She tried to stand, but wound up falling to her knees, holding her chest.

I ran over and kneeled along the side of her. "Mama, what's wrong? Talk to me!" I moved her hair out of her face and looked into her pure brown eyes that were wide open, yet unseeing.

She started to shake within my grasp, coughing repeatedly before the white bubbles formed inside of her mouth. It looked like she'd eaten a bunch of soap and the suds were spilling out of her orally. The coughing intensified, along with the kicking of her legs.

Now there were tears streaming down my face. "Mama! Mama! Please!" I cried, before laying her on her back, pulling out my phone and calling an ambulance. The whole time I talked to them on the phone, my mother continued to shake and seize on the floor with roaches crawling all around her convulsing body.

I crawled back over to her and held her in my arms as she continued to shake and choke for the next five minutes. Then, all at once, her soul left her body.

By the time the ambulance arrived, I'd already given all my dope to Keyonna and cleaned up my mother's works. The emergency technicians came into the house and kneeled beside her. The first thing the white lady did was take two fingers and place them to the side of my mother's neck. She looked over to the other technician, a short, stubby Indian man, and shook her head.

He lowered his eyes and pursed his lips in sympathy. "I'm sorry, but it looks like she's already gone," he said handing the kit over to the white lady.

She pulled out a syringe and filled it with Narcan. She flicked the syringe before picking up my mother's arm and injecting solution. The man placed the pads on her chest that could revive her heart. He hooked them up to some sort of a machine and turned it on after the white lady pulled the syringe out of her arm.

I watched the pads pull at her chest, causing it to rise. Her body jerked upward but there was still no positive response. I blinked tears and swallowed my spit, feeling like I was about to die alongside of my mother. I felt like I was the blame.

The technicians continued to go to work on her. The whole time I felt sicker and sicker, until finally I had to stand up, and in the doorway of the apartment so I could inhale the fresh air that breezed its way inside. I took deep breaths, looked out into the night and made eye contact with Keyonna as she sat in the passenger's seat of my 87' Chevy Caprice Classic. She wiped tears from her face and lowered her head.

"I got a pulse! I got a pulse! It's faint, but it's there!" the female technician yelled, just as a big fire truck pulled in front of the house, right behind my car.

They unloaded and ran up the porch steps, right past me and inside. My heart skipped beat after beat as I watched them load my mother onto a stretcher, and out of the house, into the back of the ambulance.

***

Two hours later, me and Keyonna found ourselves sitting in the waiting room of the intensive care unit of Mount Sinai hospital in Milwaukee, Wisconsin, preparing to receive the worst possible news that we could have about our mother's condition.

Keyonna laid her head on my shoulder. "I'm getting sleepy, Rich. I hope she's okay in there," she said before exhaling loudly.

I rubbed her soft cheek before kissing her on the forehead. "We know that mama is a fighter. I ain't worried about her pulling through this battle. It's what happens after this win what I'm worried about." I said, pulling her firmly into my embrace.

"Rich, even if she do pull through, which I know she will, I still don't want to live with her anymore. I can't take it. I feel like something bad is going to happen to me under her care, plus I can tell that she hates me now. It's common sense. I miss our dad," she whispered.

Just then the doctor appeared into the waiting room. He and I made eye contact and he waved me over.

I kissed Keyonna on the forehead once again. "Hold on, ma. Let me go see what this doctor talking about," I said, rising with butterflies in my stomach.

The waiting room had about ten other people inside of it besides me and Keyonna. Out of the ten, seven of them were fast asleep and the other three were looking around as nosey as news reporters.

When I got to the hallway, the doctor extended his hand and I shook it reluctantly. Our eyes me, and he gave me a look that told me he was about to give me some unfortunate news. I felt my knees get weak in preparation for it.

He took a deep breath and slowly blew it out. "Well, these things are never easy to tell a family, so I'm going to

16

come right out with it," the older white man said with the blue hospital mask around his neck.

I swallowed. "Alright, just give it to me like it is. No sugar coating." I looked him in the eyes.

He broke our eye contact and looked at the floor. "I'm sorry to tell you that your mother expired twenty minutes ago, after falling into cardiac arrest."

It seemed like the entire world stooped, and suddenly I had been thrown into a furnace. Sweat poured from my forehead and all down my back. My own heart was beating so fast that I couldn't breathe. I took two steps back and bumped into a stretcher that was in the middle of the hallway. I shook my head with my eyes wide open in disbelief. "Nah, not my mother, man. My mother is a fighter. She can come from under anything. You telling me that she had a heart attack and died?"

The doctor stepped forward and nodded his head. "Yes. Well, she had a heart attack that was brought on by extremely high blood pressure, and she over dosed today off one of the most potent versions of heroin that we'd seen. I'm sorry for your loss, son. We're going to need for you to claim the body and to make further arrangements."

That entire day continued to replay itself over and over inside of my mind's eye a week later as I stood, watching my mother's casket being lowered into the ground. She was buried on March 21st of 2018.

HOOD RICH

Chapter 2

My mother had a really good friend by the name of Andrea that she'd went to high school with, and they'd basically grown up alongside one another, even though Andrea was four years younger than her. My mother and Andrea had been really close for a long time, until my mother met my father, and he'd ultimately turn her out on heroin. After that took place, my mother withdrew into herself, and therefore her relationship with Andrea became estranged. However, after my mother passed away, Andrea was the only person willing to take in my sisters and myself. I promised her that I would do all that I could to help her out with the bills, and she said that she'd hold me to it. Andrea, was 5'4" and golden colored with long, curly hair that fell to her waist. She was Puerto Rican and Black and was thick as hell with a big ass booty. I knew that staying with her was going to be a problem for me because I secretly liked her so much.

***

One day, after I came back from dropping my sister's off at school, Andrea met me at the front door, dressed in some tight, red boy shorts that were stuffed all the way up into her kitty lips. Her thick thighs were exposed, along with her pretty toes that were painted red and black. She wore a black tank top that was so tight that I could make out her thick nipples on each breast. Her lips were shining from the MAC lip gloss that she had glazed them with.

As I stepped inside and closed the door, she smiled and took a step back, holding a hand behind her back. I lowered my eyes and looked her over from head to toe, unable to mask my fascination with her body. I couldn't believe she was so bad. That shit was blowing my mind. We'd been staying with her for about a month, and every time I saw her walking around the house in next to nothing I always did my best to avert my eyes, because deep down she caused feelings inside of me to stir that I didn't understand. This was my mother's high school friend, so not only did I feel guilty for some of the thoughts that I had about her, I also felt intrigued.

I hung my jacket on the rack and looked down at her with a curious expression on my face. "What's good with you Andrea?"

She smiled, biting into her bottom lip before running her tongue all over them. "I got something for you. I think it's time that you get out there and really get yo' weight up." She came from behind her back with a stack of money and handed it to me. "Here. I want you to flip this shit and get on yo' feet. I can't have you staying in this muhfucka if you ain't bringing in no real paper."

I took the money and started to count through it. "How much is here?" I asked, raising my thick right eyebrow, looking down on her.

She sucked on her bottom lip all sexy like, popping back on her legs. "That's fifteen gees right there. You should be able to cop something real nice with that. I'm expecting you to have my fifteen back to me in two weeks. If you can do that, then I'll be able to hit you with fifteen or more every other week, until I don't need to do it no more. I wanna see you do your thing, and since you the only man in this house, you ain't got no other choice." She smiled up at me, even though I could tell that she was dead serious.

I nodded my head looking down at the money, already knowing which one of the homies I could holler at to get right. I started to imagine the possibilities, and it got me a lil' excited 'cuz I was ready to get on my feet and to start spoiling my sisters. I was tired of seeing them walking around with the same two outfits that they had for damn near six months. Prior to Andrea hitting me with the money, I was only making enough in the slums to cover my mother's rent and bills. After she passed away, it was more of the same for Andrea's. After I put up my end for her bills, I was left with peanuts. So, I was forced to watch my sisters walk around all bummy and shit.

Andrea stepped into my face and stood on her tippy toes, looking me in the eyes. "You don't seem like you're happy at all. I thought with me hitting you with this lil' chump change it'd give you a boost in the game. You know I can't depend on Maxwell." She rubbed the side of my face.

Maxwell was Andrea's boyfriend. I guessed he hustled a lil' bit on the east side of town and had a few urban clothing stores, but from as far as I could tell he really wasn't the type to trick off his paper on her. The nigga was real funny acting. One of them swearing up and down he was a pimp-types.

I felt her hot fingers on my face and the feel of them was causing me to feel some type of way. She held me with her small left hand, looking from one of my eyes onto the next, sucking her bottom lip the entire time. I felt jittery. I hated that Andrea was so damn fine.

"Nah, I was just thinking about how I was going to make it happen with this bread, that's all."

She smiled and leaned in close enough so that her nose was touching mine. "Rich, I make you nervous, don't I?" She whispered.

The smell of her perfume sailed up my nose, intoxicating me. She was so fine that I was finding it hard to look her in the eyes. "What? Hell n'all. I'm good." I shifted my weight from one foot onto the next, lying my ass off. Every time I knew that her and I were alone in the house it made me feel uneasy.

There I was, eighteen years old, trying to figure life out, and there she stood— this grown ass woman, obviously about that life.

She wiggled her nose against mine, looking into my eyes. "I done caught you peeping me a few times. I know you like me, Rich. You might as well go ahead and tell the truth. Ain't nobody here but us." She brushed her lips against mine before turning her head to the side and sucking them into her mouth while her hand ran all over my stomach muscles.

The next thing I knew, her hand was in my pants, feeling around for my pipe. When her hand wrapped around it she gasped, opening her eyes wide before squeezing it.

"Umm, Andrea. What you on, man?" I groaned, sucking her lips as she walked forward into me, breathing hard. I noticed that both nipples on her breasts were hard and poking through her top.

She sucked my lips and moaned into my mouth. "Grab my ass, Rich. I know you wanna touch that big ol' thang. It's good. I want to show you somethin'." She started to unbutton my jeans.

I reached my hands around and cuffed that big ass booty; squeezing it and pulling the chunky cheeks apart. I mean I knew that Andrea was strapped but looking from a distance didn't do her the justice that she deserved. Once I felt how soft and heavy that ass was, I couldn't help my pipe from sticking straight up after she uncovered it.

She pulled my jeans and boxers down at the same time, dropping to the carpet in the living room on her knees, looking up at me with want and desire written all over her face. "Umm, look, Rich. I don't mind doing what I gotta do to make sure that you hit that game hard out there. I know it's a cut throat world out there, baby, so I'll support you in any way that I can. After you cross this threshold of my house, I'mma need for you to fuck me the way that I need to be fucked, and don't worry because I'mma teach you everything that you need to know." She stroked my pipe before pulling it to her face and sniffing the head. "Umm, shit, yes."

She opened her mouth and sucked me inside, then started to spear her head on my dick, again and again. The wet sounds from her slobbering was driving me crazy. I stood with my back against the wall, moaning deep within my throat. My toes were curled, and the heat from her mouth had me on the verge of coming already.

I reached down and pulled up her tank top. I'd always been infatuated by the sights of seeing her titties bounce up and down in whatever tops she wore. Her nipples often poked through her fabrics, teasing me, even when I was just a little boy and discovering what they really were.

She stopped sucking for a moment, took her top and pulled it over her head and off her arms. "There you go, Rich. You can finally see my titties, baby. I know you been wanting to." She sucked me back into her mouth and really got to doing her thing.

I watched her titties jiggle and had to close my eyes because I was seconds away from cumming. "Shit, Andrea, slow down. I can't hold this back. Slow down, please. I can't handle this head."

Those words must've motivated her to go harder, because the next thing I knew she was stroking my dick with one hand and sucking the soul out of me. The slurping noises were so loud in my ears that I could no longer hold back.

"Uh! Uh! Shit! Here it come! Uhh, ummm-uh!" I grunted as she stroked my piece rapidly. My body tensed up. I felt my balls go into my stomach, and then I was shooting off like a squirt gun, again and again while she sucked me harder.

"Look at me, Rich." More sucking accompanied the loud slurping noises. She popped my dick out of her mouth and stroked it up and down as my cum flew out of me and onto her tongue and lips. She continued to stroke. "Look at me, baby. I love this shit!" She sucked me back into her mouth.

My knees buckled. I was so weak, yet at the same time my dick continued to stand up hard as a rock. I wanted to be in her body. I needed to hit that grown pussy. I'd been feening for her ever since I was a lil' kid and couldn't believe that my fantasy was becoming a reality.

She popped my piece out of her mouth and stood up, sliding her hand into her panties, before pulling them down and from her ankles. Once they were off, she lifted her small foot and placed it on the couch, looking at me with lust in her eyes. Her fingers ran over her bald, golden sex lips that were a shade darker than her skin. She opened the lips, exposing her pink insides that glistened from her juices. "Rich, I want you to eat me, baby. I need you to lick up and down this slit, and then suck on this thing right here." She pulled her lips all the way back and pointed at her thick clitoris.

My dick was so hard that it was jumping up and down, throbbing. I wanted to taste her so bad that I felt like hollering that shit to her. I damn near broke my neck coming over and kneeling before her. She took the back of my head and pushed my face into her box. She humped into my mouth as I extended my tongue and licked up and down her wet slit. Her juices drenched my nose and dripped from my chin. Her clit stuck out so far that it looked like a third nipple. I sucked it into my mouth and ran my tongue back and forth across it.

"Un! Un! Un! Yes, baby! Eat me! Uhhh, it feel so good baby!" She moaned loudly, grabbing her titties and pushing them together.

Both nipples stood out a cool inch after she got done pulling on them. Her kitty smelled just a little sweaty, and that turned me on even more because it was her natural scent. I licked up and down as if I was going crazy, slurping just as loud as she was when she was sucking me off.

"Uhh! Uhh! Rich! Lil' daddy! You finna make me cum! You finna make me cum, Rich! Uhhhh!" She grabbed my head and started to ride my face while I held her thick ass cheeks, moving my face from side to side, loving the sounds she made above me. The taboo aspect of it all. "Uhhhhh!" She screamed, before cumming all over my mouth, nose, and chin. Her body shook continuously. She pushed me back and bent over the couch. "Fuck this shit, Rich. I need you to put that dick in me. I don't care who you are to me, or what nobody gotta say about what we doing. This is between us; family business." She smacked her ass and spread her legs wide.

I watched her pussy pop out from the back with its lips open and oozing her cream that tasted better than forbidden fruit. I kneeled and kissed each lip before standing up and placing my dick head at her pink hole. Then, I slid in with so much force, feeling the heat and the tightness of her womb swallowing me whole.

"Uhhhh, shit, yes! Yes, baby! Now fuck me. Pull back as far as you can without letting your dick slip out, and slam forward into my box like you're mad at me. Don't play with my pussy, Rich. Don't no woman like that. Fuck me like you trying to prove a point and I'll be your slave. Trust me on this." She bent all the way over the arm of the couch, forcing her ass to open. I could see the crinkle of her backdoor.

I grabbed her hips and slammed forward as hard as I could, pulled back and did it again.

"Umm, shit!"

Her pussy was so good. Her juices ran down my thighs from our connection of sex parts. I got to fucking her with anger, trying to match the intensity that she demanded.

"Uh! Uh! Uh! Uh! Yes! Yes! Fuck me, Rich! Ooo-a! Fuck me harder! Own this pussy! You see all this ass! Uhh-a! I need this big ass dick! Fuck a break! I need it so bad!" She moaned out.

Her ass slammed back into my lap, jiggling like jello. At the same time her titties bounced back and forth.

The scent of our romp floated into the air and up my nose, giving me motivation to dig deeper and deeper. I reached forward and took a hold of her right breast, feeling the hard nipple poke the palm of my hand. I couldn't believe that I was finally able to touch her there. The reality of it all was enough to drive me mad with lust. I pinched the nipple and pulled it away from her tit. This caused her to slam back harder into my lap, sucking my pipe through her vagina.

"I'm cumming on this dick, Rich! I'm cumming on you, baby. Ooo-a, this shit ain't right. We ain't, supposed to be doing this! Uhhh-a! Shit, fuck, yes!" She screamed.

I was fucking her so hard that every time her big ass flew backward and crashed into my abs, it felt like a gut punch, but the pussy was so good that it made me speed up the pace. "This my pussy! This mine! Tell me!" I hollered, feeling myself.

"Unnn! Shit!" She whimpered, looking over her shoulder at me with tears in her eyes. Her head bounced around on her neck as I continued to plow into her like a savage. The sound of our skins slapping together was like somebody was clapping their hands together for an encore.

"Tell me!" I hollered. Her walls sucked at me. I didn't think I could last that much longer. That pussy was too hot and tight.

"Uh! Uh! You. Fucking. The shit. Out. Of me. Rich! Oooo-a, baby! It's yours! I swear to God! Uhhh! I'm cumming!" She shrieked and began to shake like crazy, slamming backward into me.

I felt her walls vibrating. She screamed my name and then slumped to the floor with me still on top of her, fucking away while my seed came spilling out of me and into her. I pulled out of her pussy and came all over that big ass booty. I rubbed my dick head all over it, still in disbelief that Andrea had let me fuck after so many years of lusting after her.

After we were finished, we laid there on the carpet for a while, naked, while she rubbed and kissed all over my stomach, and licked along my waistline before climbing up my body and laying her head on my shoulder. "Rich, I need you to get out there and get money, baby. Life is too hard, and you're this family's only hope of making shit happen. This lil' job I got is just enough to keep us skating by. It ain't enough for me, it ain't enough for you, and it ain't enough for your sisters." She reached down and grabbed my pipe, squeezing it.

I felt it rising in her hand and knew that I was in trouble. Everything about Andrea turned me on. I didn't give a fuck about our relation or the fact that she was eleven years older than me. "Whatever I gotta do to make it happen for this family, I am. You ain't gotta worry about me sitting on my ass and watching y'all go without. That ain't in me. I know what I gotta do, so just trust me enough to know that I'mma do it." I leaned down and kissed her cheek.

She smiled and looked up at me. "Don't be trying to fall all in love with me and shit. This ain't about all that. I just know that the only way you can get a man's attention is if you get the attention of his dick first. After you conquer him sexually, a woman will be able to communicate with him intellectually. That's just how it is." She sat up on her elbows and looked into my hazel eyes that were given to me by my Italian father, before rubbing my cheek. "You do got me feeling some type of way though. I didn't know you could get down like that." She kissed my lips, then rubbed my cheek against her own before jumping up and helping me to come to a standstill. She stepped forward and wrapped her arms around my neck, looking up at me. "I meant what I said though. I need you to go out and make it happen. You got three women in this house that need you to do exactly that, so handle yo' business."

TRAPHOUSE KING

Chapter 3

When it came to fucking with niggas on that kicking it tip, I didn't get down like that because I had this thing in me that naturally hated other dudes for whatever reason. I felt like a lion. I needed to have my own Pride, and I didn't want other males anywhere near my vicinity. There was only one nigga that I kicked it with, and his name was Demetrius, but everybody in the hood, including myself, called him, Paper.

I met Paper when I was in the fourth grade and me and him had got into over this girl named Tasha that we both liked. I thought that she was my girlfriend and only mine, but it turned out that she was going out with both me and Paper. Long story short, one day at recess she told us that we had to fight and whoever won would get her as a consolation prize. Being young and naive, along with all our class mates geeking us up, me and Paper went head up three times that recess. I won the first fight, and he won the second. By the third fight we were both out of breath and did a lot of wrestling, so I can't really say who won that one, but Tasha wound up choosing me, and I was cool with that, until I found out that she was still messing around with Paper on the side.

People usually wondered how much fourth graders really could do at that age. All I could say was that reality would blow their minds.

One of the reasons we were fighting over Tasha is because she was an advanced lil' girl.

I would go in the bathroom with her during school hours and every single time she'd show me something new sexually that kept me hooked. One day as I was coming out of school with my arm wrapped around her, and there was

Paper in a circle of boys. They were acting like they were about to jump him, so they could take his Air Jordan's that his father had sent him from the joint. He always bragged about his old man being locked down in Waupun Maximum Security Prison out there in Wisconsin, and still being able to send him home stacks of money every month. So, as I was coming out of the school, Paper was takin his shirt off.

"Yo, I ain't scared of none of you niggas. Y'all want my shoes you gon' have to kill me!" he hollered, then swung and punched a heavy-set sixth grader in the jaw, knocking him to the ground.

As soon as he fell, two boys swung and punched him at the same time, knocking him backward. But that didn't stop Paper from swinging with calculating blows. The dark-skinned kid went for what he knew. His heart was bigger than the average.

All the boys closed in and started to attack him at once, getting the best of him, and that infuriated me. I already didn't like bullies, but worse than that I hated cowards that had to group up before they fought. That was my pet peeve, and the middle school that we went to was known for that. I hated Auer Avenue.

I took my arm from around Tasha as the rest of the kids started to come out of the school doors talking loudly as if they could not wait to be free. As they made their way completely out of the school they all peeped what was going on with Paper and the six other boys.

Paper was on the ground getting stomped out by all six of them. I ran over as fast as I could and got to swinging, hitting one face after the next. I mean hard too. They must've been taken off guard because every time I connected with one of their faces the culprit would run away until he gathered himself. "Get off him!" I hollered, still swinging.

After I cleared the way a lil' bit, Paper was able to get up and place his back to mine, and that day we stood back to back, fighting off all six of the dudes until the teachers and bus drivers came over and broke us up. My lip and nose were bloody, along with Paper's, but he didn't lose his shoes. The only thing I had left behind was Tasha. Simultaneously, I gained a best friend and the only man I trusted with my life.

Nine years later and me and Paper were even closer than we were back then. I drove over to 26th and Burleigh where Paper's trap was and parked my car behind his black on black Monte Carlo that his father had brought him while he was in the joint. I got out of my whip and made my way along the gangway of his trap with the sun beaming down on my head. It felt extremely humid outside, and even though I was wearing Polo shorts and a gray and black Polo wife beater over matching Air Max 95's, it did little to keep me cool. Before I made it to the back of his trap I had sweat pouring down the side of my face, and my beater was sticking to me just that fast.

When I got back there, I found Paper down on one knee, shaking dice, getting ready to roll them out of his hand. He looked up at me and smiled. "Rich! What's good, my nigga? You just in time to watch me break these fools," he said as a slight breeze coursed through his backyard.

Alongside Paper was four other dudes, all with money in their hands and their eyes on the pile of cash in the middle of them. I walked over to the circle and I could see a few of them sizing me up. More than likely they were assessing the threat that I posed to them. Around this time Milwaukee county was packed with jack boys. You never knew who was out to lay yo' ass down, but I wasn't on that shit. I had hustling on my mind. I wasn't trying to gain a bunch of new enemies, so I came over and kneeled beside Paper as he shook the dice and rolled them out into the circle.

They fell on the number nine. He pulled out a knot and peeled off a fifty. "Yo, I'll straight nine for fifty. I'm taking all side bets," he announced, looking the men over.

All around they began to fade his bet, and for every man that pulled out a fifty, Paper placed a fifty on top of theirs. I was curious to know where he'd gotten that knot from. It looked like it was well over ten bands.

Paper smiled and ran his tongue across the front of his teeth, looking from one man onto the next. There must've been eight men that faded his bet at fifty dollars apiece. I calculated that if he hit his point he'd been able to pick up four hundred dollars real quick. All he had to do was roll a nine on the dice and avoid hitting the number seven and he would be good.

He nodded. "Yo, on everything, this the easiest money I ever made." He turned the dice over in his hand before placing them side by side and shaking them furiously. He started to laugh to himself. "Y'all ready?" He asked looking around at the circle of men.

One dude with long corn rows and a mouth full of gold sucked his teeth loudly. He held a hand full of fifties and hundreds. He swatted a fly away from his face and looked over at Paper. "Man, nigga, roll the muthafuckin' dice. It's too hot to be playin' these games with you, shorty." Sweat slid down his forehead and disappeared into the collar of his buttoned-up Marc Jacobs.

Paper laughed out loud and looked him over. "Fax, chill, nigga. I ain't never seen a muhfucka in a rush to lose they money." He laughed again then looked over to me. "Watch this shit, Rich. it's like taking candy from a baby." Looking into the center of the gamble, he shook the dice close to his ear as if he was listening to them. "Here come that nine, homeboys. Sss, get 'em." He rolled the dice into the circle. They went about five feet in front of him, turning over and over before falling on a five and a four. The men in the circle seemed to let out a loud groan in unison while Paper laughed out loud. "Hell yeah. Give me my money, then I'm fading all shooters."

One by one, he went around the circle picking up one fifty at a time, leaving down the fifty that he'd originally placed with each man. "I'll bet back with all of you niggas. Fades up right now."

Not to be out done, each one of the men that had faded him before placed another fifty on top of the one that he'd left down in front of them. So once again it looked like Paper was placing another four hundred-dollar bet, after stuffing the previous cash into his pocket.

He shook the dice once again over his head. "This shit so sweet. Watch this, homie." He shook them harder as the wind blew across the backyard, lifting some of the cash before the men caught the bills in the air and set them back on the concrete, placing a rock on top of each bet to hold it to the ground. "Yeah, my niggas, read these bitches and weep!" He rolled the dice out in front of him. They twirled over and over until they stopped on a six and a five. Paper jumped up and got to collecting his bets. "Ha-ha! I told you niggas. Y'all can't fuck with my business! I'm getting all in that ass." He collected all his cash from them, once again leaving a fifty in front of each man so they could fade his new bet.

All of them, except for Fax, shook their heads and backed away from the circle.

"This nigga lucky today, kid. I ain't fucking with him. I gotta hit the block and get back what I lost." A heavy-set dark-skinned dude said, pulling out his iPhone and texting.

"Word up! I'm with you. Let's go get money. We'll holla at you niggas," another one said, walking out of the backyard with two pistols clearly showing, tucked safely into the small of his back.

Seeing them made me feel a lil' apprehensive because Milwaukee county was frivolous for jack boys. I didn't think Paper was too worried, or at least he didn't act like he was.

He was too busy sizing up Fax, who was on one knee with a bundle of cash in his hand. "Yo, so what's it gon' be, Fax? What you trying to do?"

Fax was one of the hustlers from Center Street. He was part of a local street mob by the name of CSG. They call themselves Center Street Gangstas. They were a small crew of hustling savages that trapped all throughout the city, but mainly on Center Street. They mostly sold crack and heroin, but around that time they were also venturing out into the meth market. Hustling wasn't the only thing they were known for, because while their crew was mostly made up of dope boys, they also had a bunch of jack boys, and some cats that you could hire to body a nigga for you at ten gees a murder. In so many words, Fax wasn't the nigga to play with because he was plugged in every sense of the word. His brother JG was head of CSG and he gave Fax a lot of leeway.

Fax mugged Paper then grunted before counting through his wad of money and throwing down ten one hundred-dollar bills. "Nigga, shoot a gee. Fuck playing around with that baby money." He sucked his teeth loudly and I noticed his guy looking me over closely like he was on bullshit or something.

Paper laughed and shrugged. "Nigga, you ain't said shit but a word. What I'm supposed to be scared to bet on me?" He snickered. "Yeah, right." He pulled out his knot of cash, counted out a stack and threw it on top of Fax's gee, then counted off ten more one hundred-dollar bills and tossed them down on top of the money. "Fuck a gee, shoot two."

Fax curled his upper lip and bit into his bottom lip, counting off ten more hundred-dollar bills before tossing them down. "Shoot, nigga." He ordered Paper.

Paper shook the dice in his hand above his head, laughed and looked over to me. "Watch me finish stripping this nigga. Get 'em, girls!" he rolled at the dice and snapped his fingers as they left his hand.

The dice twirled a few times before landing on two number twos. Paper grunted and shook his head, going into the circle and picking the dice up with a worried look on his face.

Fax was smiling at this point, counting through his wad of money. "Yeah, nigga." He counted off fifty-one hundred-dollar bills. "That's five bands right there, plus the two that's already down, making it seven. I say you don't straight four for this five. What you wanna do?" he asked, looking over to Paper.

Paper rolled the dice around in his hand, looking off into the distance. "I'll ten and foe. That straight foe gon' be hard to come by. All craps kill," he uttered, meaning that he'd bet Fax for that extra five gees that he'd be able to hit the number ten or four before the dice rolled on to any of the crap numbers that were snake eyes— the numbers twelve and three or seven.

Fax laughed and shook his head. "N'all, nigga. I want that straight four. In fact." He counted off another ten one hundred-dollar bills. "I'll put up six gees saying that you can't hit it. You in or you out?" he asked, running his tongue across his teeth.

Paper rolled his head around on his shoulders as the sun continued to beam down on all of us.

I hated the fact that his backyard didn't provide any shade. I was hot as hell and getting crazy vibes from Fax's man that kneeled to the left of him.

Paper counted his knot that was real thin by this point. "Yo, all I got is six hundred left, but I ain't scared. I'll put up this six and you just take four hundred back." He dropped the six hundred dollars on the pile and started to shake the dice in his hand, ready to roll them.

Fax frowned. "All you got left is six? Word up?"

Paper scrunched his face and nodded. "Yeah, just take four back and we good." He kneeled, getting into his shooters stance.

Fax shook his head, reached into the circle and started to push all the money together into one pile. "N'all. Then all of this is me. We already stipulated that the shooter had to fade whatever the fader wanted him to shoot. Because yo' money lacking, lil' nigga, you burnt yo' money, which means that all of this is mine." He kneeled and got to picking it up.

Paper reached and grabbed a chunk of it out of his hand. "You got me fucked up, homeboy. It ain't going down like that!"

Fax backed up, and the nigga that had been kneeling to the left of him stepped forward and placed a .45 to Paper's head. "Bitch ass nigga, you heard what he said. You burnt yo' money, now fall back while he collect what's his." He pressed the barrel even harder into Paper's forehead and twisted it sideways.

Seeing the way my mans had his head tilted backward, caught off guard, got me vexed. I jumped up, ready to attack even without a pistol, and that's when Fax upped a nine-millimeter and cocked it back. "Fuck you think you finna do, lil' nigga? Huh? Put yo' muhfucking hands up, now!" he hollered.

I slowly put my hands up about shoulder length while I mugged the shit out of Fax, and then his homie. They'd caught us slippin' and I felt like a straight pussy. "Man, it ain't gotta go down like that. My nigga gon' put up six and I'm gon' toss on the other four, so he ain't burnt shit. It's good money all around the board," I said looking from Fax to his shooter.

Fax scrunched his eye brows and then smiled. "Aw, you saying you got four hundred on you right now?"

As soon as he asked the question I felt dumb as hell because I felt what he was getting ready to do, but like I fool I nodded. "Yeah, and I'll back him. So, what's good?"

Fax tilted his head back and laughed. "Nigga, fuck that. Y'all done already made me sweat my deodorant off. I'm stripping you and him. Lay it the fuck down, now!" he said, walking over to me and pressing the barrel of his gun to my cheek, pushing me up against the back of the house and turning my pockets inside out until he uncovered the five thousand dollars of Andrea's money that I'd brought with me to cop some heroin from one of Paper's plugs.

After he recovered the money I felt so sick that I almost threw up on this nigga.

Fax turned me around until I was facing the house, then he put his forearm into the back of my neck all aggressive like and put his lips on my ear. "This what you get for fucking with this nigga Paper. Every time I see y'all together, I'm gon' make you and him pay for it. This nigga talk way too much, so this what it is." He pushed me into the house one last time before they forced us to kneel onto the concrete at gunpoint, and then our stomachs.

We stayed that way until they left out of the backyard and pulled out of the alley. By that time, I was so heated that my eyes were burning.

Chapter 4

I jumped up from the concrete as I heard their tires screeching down the alley in a haste to get away from the scene.

Paper jumped up and dusted his clothes off, shaking his head. "That bitch ass nigga dawg. I knew he was on somethin'. I should have known that nigga couldn't take no L's," he said lowering his head.

I was pacing, heated. My eyes felt like they were about to drop tears. Andrea had just given me that money, so I could make a way for the family, and I had already lost half of it. I got to imagining the faces of my little sisters and then hers, and I felt like I had the flu. Like I had failed them already. I shook my head. "Yo, I ain't finna take that loss lying down, Paper. Fuck that. I know who he pulled with and all of that, but that nigga gon' have to kill me. That money was for my lil' sisters, man."

Paper opened the backdoor to his trap and stepped inside of it. "Come in, Rich, so we can figure this shit out. You ain't gon' do shit but pass out in this sun. Word up." He stepped to the side, so I could enter, which I did.

Five minutes later I was still pacing in his living room when he entered with a snubbed nose .38 Special in his hand. He walked up to me and extended the gun. "Here, bruh, you gon' need this muhfucka later."

I grabbed it and popped open the cylinder, spinning it, making sure that each of the chambers were filled with bullets before snapping it closed. "What you got in mind, Paper? What? We finna go pop this nigga or something? 'Cuz if we is, I'm down." I said still heated.

I wanted to kill something even though I never had before. I felt like I could take Fax's life with no hesitation.

I kept on imagining what it felt like to have that steel up against my cheek and forehead and it began to make me feel crazy. I wanted to cry and scream out in anger all at the same time. I felt emasculated to the ninth power.

Paper shook his head. "N'all. I ain't saying we about to body this nigga. He gon' get his when the time is right, but for now, my old man put me up on this other lil' lick that we can hit to get our money back. It's supposed to be about a brick and a few gees, but we gon' have to hit that shit first thing in the morning. I'm talking like four or five-ish. You down?" He asked, taking a blunt off the table in the living room and lighting it. He took four deep pulls then passed it to me.

I took it, even though my chest was heaving because I was so heated. All I kept on seeing was me blowing Fax's brain out of his skull. I couldn't believe that he'd just treated me and Paper like bitches. I felt like he just screwed me or something. I had to get my revenge, or I would never be able to live with myself. However, I had that evil shit on my mind. I also couldn't stop thinking about how much my little sisters needed me. I had to step up to the plate and get them right, along with Andrea. I was the man of the house and the only hope they had.

I took three quick pulls from the blunt and watched him crush up two Percocet thirty pills, sit at the table and snort them line by line. He pinched his nose and coughed more than a few times. I wasn't fucking with them pills at this point, but Paper was into them real heavy. I took the gun and put it into the small of my back. Then, I puffed away at the blunt, feeling the high take over me. My eyes got low and time seemed to slow all the way down. "Tell me what's good with this lick, Paper? What's the risk?" I asked, really not caring. I was willing to do whatever it took to make it happen for my household.

Paper tooted up another line and sat back in his chair with his eyes glossed. He took three Jolly Ranchers and popped them into his mouth, sucking loudly. "Look, bruh, trust me. We gon' get that nigga Fax. I'm just as heated as you, even though it may not seem like it, but for right now we need to make other moves. It's this rock house ran by this skinny Mexican nigga on the south side that we can hit. His father two cells over from my Pops in the joint, and my old man just put him in with a seller that dropped a kilo of white on him. He's supposed to be buying two pistols tomorrow afternoon which is why we gotta hit his ass before he do. He just got the dope last night, so it's good. My old man gave me all the details on our visit yesterday. I guess the lil' nigga trying to raise money to get his pops a good lawyer. Unfortunately, we gon' have to put a delay on all of that. We need this bread and that work." He blew his nose into a Kleenex, opened it and looked inside before balling it up and tossing it on the table.

From a distance I could see a lil' blood. I wondered if that was normal for tooters. I exhaled loudly. "Man, look. I gotta get that cash back, so if we ain't finna go right at Fax ass then I'mma ride beside you on this lick, just as long as we splitting this shit down the middle."

Paper scooted his chair away from the table and stood up on wobbly legs. Stepping forward a little unbalanced, he opened his arms for me to step inside of them. "Nigga, you already know we eat off the same plate. Everything I have is yours. I love you, boy!"

I looked him up and down, trying to calm my anger, feeling the remnants of our attack by Fax and his shooter. I stood there for a few seconds, not feeling like hugging my nigga, even though I loved him just as much. I thought about all that we had been through, and how through it all we'd always had each other's back.

I knew for a fact that Fax would never get away with what he did to us, and that we'd get his ass back, and make him pay in a sadistic fashion. For now, we had to focus in on getting some immediate paper.

***

Thirteen hours later I stood on the side of the Mexican's dude's house as Paper placed one of his Jordan's into my clasped hands. I lifted him up into the bedroom window that we'd pried open with the use of a screw driver. It slowly began to drizzle outside before the rain was coming down in a steady pour, leaving me drenched within minutes. The ski mask that I wore over my face stuck to it and made me feel as if there were little bugs crawling on my skin under it.

After Paper slid into the window, he helped me to hoist myself up and inside. We fell onto the floor of the small bedroom before getting up and pulling out our pistols. My heart pounded in my chest. I felt as if I had a shortness of breath, and I kept passing gas from being so nervous.

Paper waved me to follow him. We walked across the bedroom that consisted of a small bed in the middle of it, along with a brown dresser and 13-inch color television that somebody had left on the local news.

Paper reached for the door knob and slowly turned it. Pulling the door open, before sticking his head partway out of it, he looked both ways, then jerked his head back inside. "Bruh, it's dude and another nigga sitting at the table tooting lines and sipping on a bottle of Tequila. Let's bum rush they ass, get the merch and get the fuck out of here. I'm letting you know right now if I smell anything fishy, I'm bussing ASAP," he said just low enough for me to hear him.

I nodded and swallowed. I was down to do the lick one hundred percent, but I wasn't trying to catch no body over the lil' chump change that we'd come for. I mean, don't get me wrong, if I had to, I was gon' pull that trigger. I was just hoping that I could leave with the same number of bullets that I came with.

So, as the sweat poured down my back, I watched Paper slowly open the door with his gun raised, then all at once he shot out of the room with me behind him.

"Put yo' muthafucking hands in the air or I swear to God I'm knocking yo' heads off. Let's go!" he hollered.

There was one heavy-set Mexican man that had just leaned down to toot up his line of coke. When he saw us, he raised his head with eyes wide open, and looked like he was about to have a heart attack. He choked on his spit and pushed his chair away from the table, standing up with is hands in the air. "Say Vato, don't shoot, por favor. I'm just visiting."

I stepped forward and put my pistol under his chin. "Shut the fuck up and sit back down." I ordered, cocking the hammer on the .38 Special.

He nodded and sat back in the chair with his eyes closed. "Dios Mio, I don't wanna die tonight." He whimpered.

Paper snatched up the skinny, teenage looking Mexican and slammed him into the wall before putting the gun to his temple. "Check this out, Essay. I know you got a kilo of dope in this bitch and a few gees. All you gotta do is take me to the merch, and you and this old head can leave with your lives. But if you play with me, I'm stanking both of you muhfuckas. Now, where the shit at?" He asked through clenched teeth, forcing the barrel into the skinny kid's cheeks.

"Say, chill, Homes. I'll take you to it. Just get it and leave. It ain't worth dying over," he said in a calm voice.

Paper yanked him away from the wall and threw him aggressively into the kitchen, where he fell to his knees. "A'ight then, let's get to it. Lead me to the money."

The skinny kid looked up and nodded before slowly climbing to his feet, then they disappeared to the back of the house.

Meanwhile, the heavy-set Mexican man had his hands clasped together, praying out loud in Spanish. I didn't know what he was saying but it freaked me out when tears started to roll down his chubby cheeks. I felt bad for him and prayed that I didn't have to hurt him or nothing.

About three minutes later, Paper came from the back of the house with a black garbage bag in his hand, walking behind the skinny Mexican kid that he had his gun pointed to the back of his head.

The skinny kid had his hands in the air with his face lowered. "Say, Homes, that's everything. How about you get the fuck out of here now, Vato?" he uttered with a scowl on his face.

I pulled the fat one out of the chair and flung him to the floor, forcing him to lay on his stomach. "Close yo' eyes, man, and don't open them muhfuckas until I tell you to!" I hollered.

"Please, don't kill me!" he whimpered, before closing them and beginning to pray at the top of his lungs.

"Yo, we good or what?" I asked Paper.

He raised the bag and turned back to the skinny kid. "Get on yo' knees homie and lay on yo' stomach so we can get the fuck out of here."

The skinny kid lowered himself to one knee before getting onto the other one. Once there, he slowly got on his stomach and closed his eyes. "Just leave Homes. A loss is a loss."

I slowly made my way to the back of the house, opening the door wide, while Paper was saying something to him.

The next thing I knew, Paper was running toward me. "Let's go bruh, its good!"

We hit it out of the backdoor and hit it down the alley to the next block on to where Paper's Monte Carlo was parked. Once there, we jumped in and stormed away from the curb, me with a big ass smile on my face and my heart beating like an African drummer.

***

Early the next morning, we sat in Paper's trap house living room, breaking our spoils down the middle. I walked away with $4,000 and seventeen ounces of Peruvian Flake that was barely touched.

"Yo, I'mma get some sleep for a few hours, Rich, then I want you to hit me up at about one in the afternoon, so we can get on our grind. It's time to get money and get our shit together so we can go at that nigga Fax when the time is right, nah mean?" He stepped forward and gave me a half of hug.

I pat him on the back before backing up a lil' bit. "A'ight but make that like three. I gotta get some sleep too. I'm tired as hell."

As I was opening the door to the house with the black plastic bag in my hand, filled with the seven ounces of cocaine, Andrea was pulling up in front of the house after dropping off my sisters at school. She tapped the horn once then jumped out of the car, making her way up the stairs with a smile on her pretty face. The rays of the sun allowed for her light freckles to pop. I thought it made her look so sexy because I had only seen a few black females with freckles. I felt like she was a rare breed of beautiful, and every time I saw her she did something to me both mentally and physically.

"Oh, nigga, I know you tripping. You call yo' ass coming into my house at eight in the morning. We about to have a major fight. I hope you ready for it," she said, climbing the steps until she was standing in my face. Her perfume floated up my nose.

I had to close my eyes as I felt my piece hardening. She brushed past me and into the house.

I stepped inside and closed the door behind me, looking down into her brown eyes. "Aw. So, what? You gon' give me a whoopin' or somethin?" I teased, stepping forward and placing my forehead against hers.

She took a step back after pushing me just a little to create space between us. She shook her head, looking disgusted. "Look, I ain't playing, Rich. You been out there all-night long. You better have some good news or we finna have a serious problem." She scrunched her forehead and looked up to me with anger.

I scoffed. "Oh really? It's like that?" I asked, taking the bag from my right hand and grabbing it with my left. I felt a lil' odd having her charge me up like that. Like she was my pimp or something.

She crossed her arms in front of her and nodded. "It's just like that. Ain't no way you finna be on that type of shit."

I walked past her into the dining room, sat the bag on top of the table and pulled out the seventeen ounces of dope, balled up the bag and sat it in the chair. Then, I went into my pocket and pulled out the four gees that I'd gotten from the lick. "Here. These four gees right here. I got another four in the room. That'll be eight total. I'll have that other two in a day or so. I should make about forty-seven gees from this lil' seventeen zips right here, so from here on out I don't need you to give me nothing. I'mma figure everything out on my own," I said, handing her the money and making my way into the room where I laid my head while I stayed with her. Once there, I picked up the mattress and dug my hand in the hole in the box spring, taking out the ten that was inside of it. I counted out nine gees and handed it to her. "Matter of fact, here go another nine. Now, all I owe you is two. Like I said, you'll have that in a day or so."

She took the money with her eyes wide open. "Rich, look, I wasn't trying to make you feel less than a man or nothing. I should've known you was out there on your business. I'm sorry, baby. You know what?" She tossed the money onto my bed and wrapped her arms around my neck, laying her head on my chest.

Off of pure instinct, I trailed my hands down her back until I was cuffing that big ass through her mini skirt. I yanked it upward and rubbed all over her hot skin. Pulling her cheeks apart I ran my forefinger up and down her crease from the back, feeling the satin of her panties. It felt warm to the touch.

She moaned and pressed backward into my finger. "Umm, baby, here you go again."

I gripped that ass, leaned down and bit into her neck, sucking loudly while my fingers snaked their way into her leg hole. I rubbed all over her naked pussy lips. "I need to hit this pussy again, Andrea. I'm feening for it." I groaned, ripping her panties down her legs before pushing her over my bed and spreading her legs apart roughly. I unzipped my pants, pulling my boxers down, and ran my piece head up and down her wet slit.

"Uhh!" She reached behind herself and tried to push me away, but I wasn't going.

I put my forearm into her back, forcing her to the bed, took my dick and eased it inside of her hotness.

"Uhh! Get off of me, Rich! Please!" she whimpered and spread her legs further apart.

I slammed into her with brute force, took a hold of her hips, eased her off my dick, then pulled her all the way back so hard that her ass jiggled. I picked up the pace and grabbed a handful of her curly hair. *Smack, smack, smack, smack, smack, smack, smack, smack!* My pipe continued to fly in and out of her wet hole. The headboard crashed into the wall. It didn't take long for her scent to rise into the air, driving me crazy. Her hot muscle was milking me for all I was worth.

"Uh, uh, uh, uh, Rich, ooo-a, baby, baby, you, fucking me so hard again." She whimpered, sounding as if she was out of breath. "Uhh! Uhh! Uhh! Slow down. Please. Please, baby."

I yanked her head backward by the use of her hair and sped up the pace. It felt like her kitty was a fist filled with some type of hot oil. Every time she bounced back into me, I felt like I wanted to cum.

Bam, bam, bam, bam, bam, bam. Harder and harder. I was trying to reach inside of her stomach. Her titties bounced up and down inside of her Fendi tube top. They looked as if they were about to pop out. I wanted to see them again. I needed too. The sight of her nipples would send chills through me.

"Pull, that, top down, Andrea! Pull it down!" I hollered. "Damn, shit, this pussy so good, ma." I slammed into her shit and felt her pussy wrap around my pole, suffocating me.

"Ahhhh! Shit! Rich! You fucking the shit out of me!" She clenched her teeth and looked over her shoulder at me as the steady clapping of our skins resonated throughout the room loudly.

Between our legs you could hear the noise of her juices spitting all over my pipe. Her cream oozed out of her and down my leg.

I pulled out of her, picked her up and threw her back on my bed. I yanked her tube top upward, so I could see those pretty titties that had been forbidden to me my whole life. Now they were mine to do whatever to them that I pleased. I leaned down and sucked the right nipple into my mouth as I lined my dick back up and slammed into her with animal force. I was long-stroking her with all that I had, while she twisted on the bed of money.

"Rich! Rich! Awww, shit! Rich! I love you! I love you so much! Aww, shit, fuck me! Fuck meeee-a!" She screamed before sitting up and falling back down, screaming at the top of her lungs.

I took both legs and put them on my shoulders, stroking her for all that I was worth. Her pussy got wetter and wetter. I zoomed in on the way her nipples stood out from her breasts. Her titties jiggled. There was a little drool coming from the corners of her mouth. All that shit looked sexy to me. It meant that she was enjoying my body just as much as I was enjoying hers. I dug my nails into her thighs and clenched my teeth as I felt my seed getting ready to shoot out of me.

My eyes got low. I felt dizzy and happy at the same time. Then, the next thing I knew I was coming in large globs deep within her womb while she licked all over her lips and jerked under me uncontrollably.

"Arrrgh! Shit!" I hollered, slamming my hips into her center.

Her juices leaked from my pipe and dripped onto the bed sheets. As she was screaming at the top of her lungs with her eyes closed, something told me to look to my left toward the door of my bed room. When I did, my heart damn near dropped into my stomach. I almost broke my neck when pulling out of her.

Chapter 5

"You dirty bitch!" Maxwell hollered, running toward the bed with his fists balled up.

Before I could get all the way off of Andrea, he reached and grabbed a handful of her hair, yanking her head roughly.

"Ahh! Let me go, Maxwell!" she hollered in pain, popping her legs open as she tried to fight him off with her fists swinging wildly in his direction.

I fell to the floor, reached for my boxers and slipped them up my thighs before gathering myself.

He straddled her to the floor. *Smack.* "Punk bitch!" *Smack.* "You in here fucking this lil' boy!" *Smack.* "I should kill yo' trifling ass." *Smack.*

I heard Andrea yelp in pain the last time before I ran over and punched Maxwell so hard that he flew into the dresser with blood running out of his mouth. I grabbed Andrea by the arm and pulled her to her feet. "Go in your room and lock the door. I'll handle this nigga." I growled looking down on her.

Her lip dripped blood from his attacks. She nodded and slowly backed out of the room, then got stuck in the door way, looking me over nervously. "Rich, maybe he and I should talk about this. I mean, I was wrong. I should've. Watch out!"

By the time I looked, Maxwell had already tackled me into the wall with his head down. My head jerked on my neck as I crashed into the wall, leaving a big ass hole inside of it, then he was punching me in the face over and over again. *Bam, bam, bam.* Blow after blow.

"Bitch ass nigga!" *Bam, bam.* "Mind yo' muthafuckin' business!" He swung again, trying to connect with my jaw, but I ducked, and his fist contacted the wall, slamming into it hard. "Aww, fuck!" he groaned in pain.

It was all the distraction that I needed. With my nose bloodied and dripping off of my lip, I took a step back and then, with all of my strength, stepped forward and punched him square in the mouth. I knocked him into the dresser once again before I rushed him, swinging and connecting. *Bam.* One to the jaw. *Bam, bam.* One to the chin and an uppercut. He fell to one knee.

I grabbed his head and brought his face to my own knee, slamming it into it, feeling the bone crush his nose before he flew backward and passed out on the floor.

Then, I was stomping him like a bitch, over and over again. "Get. Yo'. Punk. Ass. Up. Nigga!" Afterward, I straddled him and rained down blow after blow, imagining him beating Andrea, taking advantage of her just like a coward. I completely blacked out while whooping him.

"Rich! Rich! Stop! Stop! You killing him! You killing him, Rich! Please, stop!" Andrea yelled, trying her best to pull me off of this chump.

By the time I came back to reality his blood was all between my fingers and on my chest. I shook my head then stood up, looking down on him in a state of panic. His face was completely covered in blood. His lip was the size of a boxing glove. Both eyes were puffy and closed. He groaned in pain, tried to speak, but nothing but saliva came out of his mouth.

I reached down and pulled him up by his shirt, violently, putting my forehead against his. "Listen to me, you bitch ass nigga. If I ever catch you sniffing around her again, I'ma murk you. I don't give a fuck if you take this shit out on me. I'ma man, I can handle it, but you leave this shit between me and you. She ain't got shit to do with it. You got that?" I asked, tightening my grip on his shirt.

He nodded. Five minutes later, I was throwing him off of the porch and into the grass, while the sun beamed down on the both of us. The humidity was so bad that even though I was in my boxers, I still felt suffocated. He slowly made his way to his feet and staggered to his truck. He only looked over his shoulder one time before opening the door, getting in and pulling away.

***

Thirty minutes later, and after I'd gotten out of the shower, I was met by the sights of Andrea pacing in the living room with her head down. She was mumbling something to herself that I couldn't quite make out.

I slipped into my Gucci shorts and tossed a grey Gucci wife beater on over my head, finishing the fit with a Gucci belt and matching gray and blue Air Max 95s. I grabbed my pistol off of the dresser and walked into the living room where she continued to pace. I put the .38 into the small of my back and blocked her path. "Andrea, what's wrong with you?" I asked sincerely, concerned about her well-being.

She looked like she was on the verge of a nervous breakdown.

I placed my hands on each one of her shoulders and looked into her brown eyes.

She blinked tears and took a deep breath. "Rich, he was our only livelihood. He was the only reason I was able to fuck around with that real estate out here. He paid all of my bills and made sure that I kept some money in my pocket. I know you didn't know all of that, but it was the truth. Now that he's gone, how are we going to survive? I can't take care of your sisters and you on my own. I'll lose my freaking mind. I'm just not strong enough." She whimpered before lowering her head and crying.

I pulled her to me and rubbed her back, running my fingers through her long, curly hair once again. I could still smell the scent of sex coming off of her. "Andrea, don't worry about none of that shit. I got you, ma. I got you and my sisters. I know y'all depend on me to make it happen, so I gotta do what I gotta do," I said, feeling a little defeated because I didn't feel like she believed in me. I was only eighteen and I knew she was used to fucking with baller-type niggas, but all I needed was a chance to make it happen. I just needed for her to have a little more faith. That faith would give me an extra boost of confidence that I needed to believe in myself.

She shook her head then looked up at me with tears coursing down her pretty, soft cheeks. "Rich, you gotta understand that it ain't easy out there in that game. If you trying to do your thing then you can't make any mistakes, especially if you're going to have all of us on your back. Do you understand me?" She asked, wiping her tears away.

I nodded then helped to wipe the water away from her cheek by the use of my thumbs. I hated to see a woman cry. I always had ever since I was a little kid and witnessed the way my father broke my mother down almost every single day. He would beat her into the ground so bad that she was forced to find shelter in heroin. "Andrea, I understand, and if you know the game, then all you gotta do is teach me. I'm willing to learn, then I'll take the lessons that you give me straight into the slums and make it happen for this family. I realize what's at stake here. I can't fail. There's no room for me to." I pulled her to me once again and wrapped my arms around her small frame, hugging her with love and affection.

She exhaled loudly. "Well, if you mean that, then the first thing I gotta show you is how to cook up your own dope. That way you'll keep more of your product, and you'll be able to turn a bigger profit. The worst thing a hustler can do is to have somebody else cooking up his work. You'll almost always be cheated. Your cook will keep most of your product, and step on it with baking soda or B12. So, I'ma show you how to do everything. That way you'll never have to rely on anybody else other than yourself."

The next thing I knew, we were sitting at the kitchen table. Andrea took one of the ounces of Peruvian Flakes and dumped it into an empty mayonnaise jar after boiling a pot of water on the stove. She took a can of 7Up and poured it into the mayonnaise jar along with the dope and stirred it for about five minutes before picking it up and setting the jar inside of the boiling water.

She stirred the mixture and looked over her shoulder at me. I noticed that her lip was a little big from Maxwell's attack, but she still looked finer than ever to me. "You gotta keep stirring this shit, Rich. That way this soda can break down the compounds in the dope before you add the B12 to it. You always want to make sure that your dope is as potent as it can be. It's the only way you'll take customers from other niggas. It's gon' be plenty hustlers out there selling dope. Yours has to stand out from the crowd, you understand?" She asked, looking me in the eyes.

I nodded and stepped closer to the stove. Looking inside of the pot, I could see that the dope was completely liquefied.

She continued to stir it. "Hand me that B12 from the counter," she said, turning the eye down on the stove.

I handed the already measured amount to her and watched her add it to the mix, stirring the whole time. The mixture began to bubble before she turned the fire under the pot all the way off and continued to stir it.

After doing it for another five minutes, she added some yellow food coloring, continued to stir, and then placed the mayonnaise jar inside of the sink that was filled with ice. "A'ight, we gon' let that one rock up and knock down these other sixteen zips. I wanna watch you do it now, and let's try and be done with everything before I gotta go and pick your sisters up."

Well, it didn't take long for me to catch on, and by the time she came back home with my sisters, I was done and ready to bag up the work in the basement. After she got them situated upstairs, she came down and explained to me how to break down each ounce of dope with the use of a scale.

She chopped off a chunk of crack with a sharp pocket knife and placed it on the scale. "Alright, look, Rich. Out here in Milwaukee, you should be able to make about twenty-eight hundred dollars off of each ounce. That's a hundred dollars per zip. That's ten dime bags every hundred dollars. Now, I got a few contacts that's gon' want us to sell them eight balls. Eight balls usually consist of three and a half grams, but we ain't fucking with that. We gon' sell our balls for eighty-five dollars at three grams a piece. Okay, I'll handle that, and for now you just take care of the dime by dime bags. That's that block by block shit. I ain't got no parts in that." She held up a chunk of crack. "Now, the reason I used yellow food coloring is because I wanted to make your dope stand out. This looks like cheese, and that's what they gon' start calling it. In order to survive in this game, you gotta stand out from everybody else, and your dope has to be more potent with better quality. Treat dope fiends like family members that you care about. Never look down on them because of their usage. They are human, and we all have our vices. Your goal is to establish loyalty amongst your customers, and in time the niggas you'll have work under you. It's impossible to advance in the game if you don't enter into it with a strategy, a'ight?"

I nodded, making sure I was paying close attention. "Alright then, let's bag this stuff up so you'll be ready to go tomorrow." And that's just what we did.

It must've taken us a full eight hours to get everything packaged and ready to go. By the time we were finished, I was exhausted and felt as if I was ready to pass out. I texted Paper and told him I'd get up with him bright and early the next morning. Then, I went into my room and cleaned it up to the best of my ability, before I fell out on the bed and was out like a light.

I wasn't sleep for more than four hours before Keyonna was waking me up by climbing into the bed with me, taking my arm and putting it around her body. I opened my eyes and looked into her pretty face and noticed that there were tears rolling down her cheeks.

I sat up in bed, reached and turned my lamp on, scrunching my eye brows. "Keyonna, what's the matter, lil' sis?" I reached and rubbed her soft cheek.

She shook her head. "I'm tired of them making fun of me at school, Rich. I'm tired of them calling me a burn and saying I'm a crack head's daughter." She blinked, and more tears came out of her eyes. Now she was breathing heavy, inhaling and exhaling loudly.

Her face was redder than I ever remembered. The fact that she was hurting nearly caused me to break all the way down along side of her. I felt my throat get tight. I was both angry that people were picking on my lil' sister and pissed off at myself for giving them room to. I had to make her and Kesha more of a priority. I had to get my money right. Their normalcy depended on it.

"Keyonna, baby, don't worry. I got a few bands put up. I'll take you shopping this weekend and get you right. You and Kesha, I promise." I said, laying back and pulling her down so she could rest her head on my chest.

My sister had nice sideburns that stopped at the top of her jaw line. Because we were mixed, hers were real wavy. Whenever she got down on herself, I'd always lay her head on my chest and rub one of them until she fell asleep.

She wrapped her arm around my waist and closed her eyes. "I miss mama so much, Rich. I know she wasn't the best mother in the world, but she was all that we had. It's like we don't even exist to dad. We're over here struggling and he's over there with his Italian family living like a king. It's just not fair. It's not our fault that he and mom brought us here. Why do we have to suffer?" She whispered as I stroked her side burn.

I exhaled loudly and shook my head. I had never respected my father, even though those in the underworld of narcotics did. My father was a full-blooded Sicilian and was surrounded by an army of goons that hated the black people, or any race of people that weren't Sicilian. He'd met our mother two years before I was born on a plane, coming from Italy. She was a flight attendant that he'd at one point in time found incredibly attractive. A beautiful black woman that had been forbidden for him to even glance at while he was going through the ranks of the

Luciano Mafia. But glance he did, and before the plane would land in New York, he and our mother had fallen in love at first sight. Two years later, I was born, followed by Keyonna and then Kesha.

The entire time they were dealing with each other he'd kept her a secret. He was ashamed of the pigment of her skin. He'd beat her every chance that he got and drag her so far through the mud that she would eventually turn to first cocaine and later heroin. Heroin that he happily pumped into her veins to keep her within a dreamy state of submission.

Our father had a whole other family that he catered to and spoiled rotten. A Sicilian wife, son and daughter. Though they were our half siblings, we shared no form of a relationship and barely acknowledged the fact that one another existed.

I held Keyonna firmly. "Keyonna, don't worry about him. I'll take care of you. I'll make sure that you and Kesha are well taken care of. All I ask is that you be patient and that you believe in me. I will not fail you, I promise. Do you believe me?" I asked, looking into her pretty face.

She nodded with her eyes closed. "Yes. I love you so much, Rich. I'm glad that you're nothing like our father. You're more a dad to me than he will ever be. I hate him so much for abandoning us." She rubbed my chest and got more comfortable.

The door swung inward and Kesha appeared with her sheet wrapped around her. She was a spitting image of my mother, though two shades lighter, and with hazel eyes like my own, and Keyonna's. "Dang, Keyonna, you just gon' leave me in there all by myself?" She whined, looking from Keyonna, to me.

I scooted myself and Keyonna over in the bed, making room for her. "Come on, lil' mama, you can climb in here with me too. I need your lil' snuggles," I said trying to ease her apprehension.

Kesha was a real shy and self-conscious thirteen-year-old girl. She rarely ever spoke the things that she was feeling out loud, and more often than not I had to try my best to read her mind and make sure that I didn't leave her out of the mix because Keyonna was so over bearing when it came to me. Very possessive, and jealous. And I found no problem with it because I loved my lil' sister so much, and I understood that she'd never received any unconditional love from our parents, so I felt as if it was my job to fill in the blanks that they'd left. Especially since I felt so responsible for our mother's death.

Kesha slowly walked to the bed and got on to it, climbing across it on her knees until she was lying beside me with her head on my shoulder. "Thank you, Rich. I didn't wanna be by myself," she said before yawning and closing her eyes.

I leaned down and kissed her on the forehead. I had to make it happen for my sisters. I had to make sure that they had opportunities in life that my parents never allowed for me to have. I had to be their sacrifice. I had to do everything that it would take to get them out of the ghetto and into a better position because the world didn't care about them. They were young black women, and because of our circumstances, the statistics said that they were supposed to be losers and stuck within the ghetto's death grip. But I refused to allow for that to happen. I would've rather died first.

Keyonna kissed my cheek and rubbed her face against mine. "You're the best brother ever, Rich. I love you so, so much." Then, she was lightly snoring with her mouth open.

HOOD RICH

Chapter 6

The next afternoon, I brought five ounces over to Paper's trap and we got to doing our thing. As soon as the dope fiends saw the color of my dope, it made them curious. They'd roll a rock around in their hand, looking it over suspiciously with an eyebrow raised before biting into the plastic with their teeth to see if it would numb their tongue. After it was confirmed to be real, and assumed to be highly potent, they'd purchase no less than three of my bags.

There was this one addict by the name of Shirley who was known in the hood for being a prostitute and hustler. She was 5'2", dark skinned with a real skinny body, I guessed from all of the drug use. On the first night of hustling out of Paper's trap, she came to the backdoor, beating on it as if she was crazy. At first me and Paper thought it was the police, so I snatched up my dope and ran into the bathroom, ready to start flushing it like Andrea had taught me to do, when Shirley started to call Paper's name at the top of her lungs.

"Paper! Paper! Open this door, its yo' Aunty!" She hollered before beating on it some more.

I was on my knees at this point, just about to rip open the plastic so I could dump the dope down the toilet. At hearing her call Paper's name, I stopped in my tracks and looked over my shoulder, trying to locate him.

He appeared in the bathroom doorway breathing hard. "Bruh, chill, that's just this hype named Shirley beating on the door. Let me snatch her ass up and we'll be good. She fucked up in the head," he said, twirling his finger in a circle by his temple to indicate that she was nuts.

My heart was pounding so hard in my chest that I was finding it hard to breathe. I was thinking that I must've had the worst luck in the world for the police to be raiding our trap on the first day I came through with my product. I felt a sense of relief after I heard her calling his name.

I nodded. "A'ight, bruh, go get her ass then. She making too much noise. Got me all paranoid and shit." I stood up and stuffed my dope into my briefs that Andrea insisted I wear whenever I was out hustling. She said it was easier to keep my dope concealed that way. I had to take her word for it because everything was new to me. When I was hustling heroin, I simply kept the dope in my pocket because nobody had raised the common-sense flag within me. I guess I never stopped to think about the severity of what I was doing until Andrea made it clear that I had our family on my back. They depended on me. Only then did I see the importance of me making each move with a strategy in mind.

I felt a gust of wind pour into the house as soon as Paper opened the backdoor, followed by a female's yelp, and then the door slammed back. I walked to the top of the stairs and looked down on him and saw that he had Shirley by the throat with one hand.

He picked her up and held her against the door with an evil mug on his face. "Bitch, didn't I tell you about beating on this muthafucking doe like you crazy? Huh?" He asked, tightening his grip.

She gagged and then kicked her legs that were dangling in the air. You see, Paper was a cocky, muscle-bound nigga like myself. Me and the homey would often smoke blunts and hit up his weight bench that he had in the basement. I think it weighed about two hundred or so. Never the less it had the both of us cock strong and ripped the fuck up, so Shirley's lil' ass didn't stand a chance.

"Answer me bitch!"

I came down the stairs a lil' bit and saw that her eyes were bugged out of her head. Her dark-skinned face almost the color of blue. "Yo, nigga chill the fuck out! Put her down before you kill her skinny ass!" I hollered, making my way down to them. I didn't care if she was a dope head or not, she was still a female, and I wasn't about to let my right-hand man beat up on no woman. In my opinion that was coward shit, and I couldn't respect no man that got down like that, including Paper.

He held her for a little while longer, mugging the shit out of her. Then he turned to look at me, biting on his bottom lip before letting her drop to the ground. "Fuck this bitch, bruh!"

Shirley fell to her knees, holding her neck. She took a deep breath, coughing up a thick loogey, spitting it on the floor. Her chest heaved. I could smell the musk from under her arms along with sweat. She smelled as if she hadn't taken a shower in a few weeks.

The hotter the hallway became the more I could smell her to the point that it began to turn my stomach, and not even all of that stopped me from helping her to her feet and dusting off her knees. "You okay ma'am?" I asked, looking her over closely.

She nodded, still holding her throat. "Yeah, I'm good, baby. Long as this crazy muthafucka right here stop putting his hands on me all the time. That ain't no way to treat yo' blood, Paper." She coughed up another loogey and spat it out on the floor.

Paper sucked his teeth and curled his upper lip. "What the fuck you beating on this door so hard for?" He asked, pinching his nose. "Damn you stank, Shirley. Fuck is wrong with you?" He shook his head.

She waved him off. "I wash my ass when I feel like it. After all, it's my ass." She rolled her eyes and pulled up her dirty purple summer dress, exposing the fact that she had a fanny pack around her waist.

I didn't know what was inside of it, but I was praying that she pulled her dress back down because the scent coming from between her legs was so strong that I could literally taste it. It smelled like a sweaty version of fish. That's the best way I could explain it. I was already trying to come up with a way that I could get her to shower before she went back out into the streets. Maybe a shower, and then I'd put something on her stomach. She looked so thin. I felt sorry for her.

"Yeah, whatever, Demetrius. I bet I won't stank so bad after you see all of this." She unzipped the fanny pack and pulled out a wad of hundred-dollar bills, waving them back and forth.

Just by eye balling I could tell that it was more than five gees, easily. I was hoping that Paper was gon' split that money down the middle with me. I mean, we never had a problem bussing shit down together before, but at times you just never knew. After all, we were both coming off of monetary losses.

He let go of his nose and smiled. "Aunty, you know I'm just playing with you." He laughed and tried to give her a hug.

She shook her head and pushed him away. "N'all, nigga, fuck you. You always trying to put yo' hands on somebody like I'm your child. You know damn well that if I'm beating on this backdoor it's because I'm in danger and

I need to get the fuck away from whoever chasing me. Otherwise, when have I ever?"

Paper took a deep breath and nodded in submission. "You right, TT. I should have known. I'm sorry. Now let's talk about this knot you finna spend with me."

She smacked her lips. "Just like yo' damn mama. All y'all care about is money." She licked her thumb and started to count through the hundred-dollar bills. "Well, this seven gees right here, and I'm trying to spend at least half of it as long as you talking right. So, I guess my question to you is, how much are you going to give me for thirty-five hundred?" She asked, turning her head sideways and licking her crusty lips.

Paper crossed his arms and rubbed his chin. "Yo, what you lookin' for?" He walked up the stairs and into the trap with her following close behind.

I tried to let them get a little distance away. I didn't want to walk up the stairs directly behind her because the odor coming from her body was mind numbing to put things lightly.

As they disappeared into the house, there was a knock on the door. I almost ignored it because I wanted to hurry up and get upstairs before Paper snatched up all of old girl's money. Half of thirty-five hunnit was $1,750. I needed that lil' boost 'cuz I wanted to spend a few chips on my sisters and start to hit Andrea back, even though she was hollering all she wanted me to do was pay her bills from here on out, now that she'd gotten back thirteen of the fifteen stacks.

"Who is it?" I asked through the wooden door.

"It's Ralph. I just left here about an hour ago. I want the same shit or nothing at all," he said through the door.

I switched my pistol around to the front of my pants and cocked back the hammer, slowly easing open the door until his face came into view. It was a familiar, and he in fact had been there about an hour before. "I got that same work. What you looking for, homeboy?"

He was shaking as if he was cold. "I got three hundred and these Prada leather jackets if you want 'em. You can give me a fifty piece apiece. They fresh off the rack, and in the store, they were going for eight hundred apiece." He covered his teeth with his tongue. His eyes were bucked and glossy. He smelled like motor oil and dope smoke. I could tell that he must've smoked his last rock before he came.

"Let me see them coats, homey." I opened the door a lil' more and he handed them through. I flipped on the light in the hallway and looked the leathers over real closely. They still smelled brand new.

I knew that Prada costed some money, and in time I would be able to put my sisters inside of the fabric just to prove a point to the world that called them bums. My mind was extremely materialistic because I had never had anything. It wouldn't be until after I made my first ten million dollars that my thinking started to change, and I began to understand that designer clothing was all a part of the bigger scheme to keep our people blinded and made to feel inferior. A mental case of bondage.

Just by looking over the coats I could tell that both of them would fit Keyonna and Kesha perfectly. I fixed the hammer on my gun, dug into my crotch and pulled out the bag of yellow crack rocks. I took out ten dimes for the coats and another thirty for the $300 that he had. I was thinking of giving him a deal on the three hunnit but decided against it because I wanted to have enough dope to get half of Shirley's thirty-five hundred.

After I was situated, I opened the door. "I'ma cop these coats and take care of that three hunnit that you got too. Hand me the money."

He dug into his dirty jeans and pulled out fifteen twenties, handing them to me, and then I handed him the forty dime bags before closing the door.

When I got back upstairs and into the house, Shirley was just putting a rock into her glass pipe and setting fire to it. I took the coats and placed them on the arm of Paper's living room couch, directly across from where Shirley sat. Then, I took a seat and looked her over as she inhaled deeply with her eyes wide open and her jaws puffed out.

She held the smoke for what seemed like a full minute, then blew it into the air, reached on to the coffee table, and broke another piece off of one of the rocks that Paper had given her, before shaking her head. "I don't know, Paper, this seem like the same shit to me. I don't feel no different than what I felt last night. By the way Ralph was talking, he made it seem like you had that real good shit. If that's so, then you holding out because this ain't it." She picked it up and held it at her eye as if it were a priceless diamond. "He said it was supposed to be way more yellow than this." She shrugged and stuffed another piece into her glass pipe before lighting it.

I ain't wanna step on my man's toes or nothing like that, but I could tell by the way she was talking that she wasn't about to spend that whole thirty-five hundred dollars in Paper's trap. I got to thinking she was gon' try and low ball him, and like I said before, I needed to be able to split that money down the middle with him. I got to imagining my sister's wearing the same old clothes over and over again, and that just didn't sit right with me.

I reached into my crotch and pulled out the bag of dimes, took one out and slid it across the table. It landed right next to one of Paper's dimes, nearly the same size, but mine was bright yellow. Like Andrea had said, it looked like a piece of cheese. "Try that right there, Shirley."

She was on her way to inhaling the rock that she'd already lit inside of her pipe when she stopped, looked down at my rock, took her pipe and dumped it out before breaking mine down the middle and filling her pipe with it. As soon as she had that bad boy stuffed, she took her long flame and lit the tip, inhaling hard so much so that the fire was sucked into the pipe's hole, burning the rock inside of it almost immediately. She took four deep breaths and held the smoke inside of her lungs with her eyes closed, constantly sucking it in deeper and deeper through clenched teeth.

Paper curled his upper lip and shot me an evil look, then mugged her. I didn't give a fuck. I was on a mission for my sisters, and due to the fact that Shirley was a well-known hype all throughout the slums, I knew that her word of mouth about my product would have the fiends coming out from all over the city.

After she blew the remaining smoke to the ceiling, she looked over at me with big, glossy eyes and a weird smile on her face. She unzipped her knap sack and pulled out the wad of hundreds. "I want five thousand worth of that shit right there, baby, and I want it right now." She reached and grabbed the little piece of rock that was left and stuffed it into her pipe after handing me the money.

Paper frowned and shook his head. "Hell n'all, Shirley. You my muhfucking Aunty. Let me split that bread with my nigga. You take half of his and half of mine. That's how we get down," he said, digging deep into his crotch and pulling out a Ziploc bag full of gray rocks.

Shirley inhaled the dope deep into her lungs, then blew it to the ceiling. Her glass pipe cracked, so she sat it on the table and pulled another one out of her bra. She looked at Paper from the corners of her eyes while still sitting on the love seat. "Paper, you ain't gon' tell me how to spend my money. I said I want five thousand dollars' worth of this yellow shit that he serving, and that's just that. Your dope is okay, but it's been stepped on way too much. It makes my chest hurt. Now if you and him can come to some kind of agreement, I don't care. All I'm saying is all I want to leave with is that shit he got, period." She looked over at me and smiled.

Before it was all said and done, I gave her five gees worth of the product and wound up giving Paper five hunnit of it just for letting me serve his aunt, even though I didn't have to. I just didn't want him feeling some type of way.

After Shirley left, Paper turned to me and asked me if I could teach him how to cook his dope the right way, and of course I did. The next four hours were spent with us popping the last of his dope and me teaching him how to cook his product the right way. By the time we were finished for the night, and both out of the dope that we had bagged up, I had made a quick $9,000 even though three hundred of it was in change. I felt accomplished and like I was on to something.

Thirty minutes after leaving Paper's Trap, I wound up making it back to the block that Andrea's house was on. As soon as I pulled on to it, my heart dropped into my stomach at what I saw.

HOOD RICH

Chapter 7

Her name was Aaliyah. She was 5'4 and weighed about 125 pounds. Brown skinned with Asian like eyes and a nice body with a fat booty that made niggas pay attention. Me and Paper went to Washington High School with her, and on the first day after seeing her we'd made a pact that neither one of us would try and get at her so that we could avoid another Tasha situation. But she was cold and so fine that I didn't know for a fact that I would be able to keep that promise, especially after I discovered that she lived on the same block as Andrea. We often saw each other on our way to school and just around the neighborhood. Every time we made eye contact, she'd always be the first to break her stare. I think that she found me just as hot as I found her, but I wasn't sure because she was bad.

She had been the head cheerleader at our school and a real nerd almost in every class that I shared with her. For me, that was intimidating because while I wasn't a dummy or nothing like that, I definitely wasn't as scholastically aware as she was.

Her house was the third one from the corner of our block, and as I was pulling on to it, I saw this heavy-set, light skinned man had her up against a black on black Navigator by her throat, hollering in her face like he'd lost his mind or something. She had tears in her eyes and was beating at his hands. She was dressed in a real small mini skirt, and every time she moved in the slightest, it caused for it to rise and it looked very indecent. Especially because I remembered her for being this real shy lil' girl with a pretty face. So, as I rolled by, I let down my window so I could hear what dude was saying.

"Bitch, I don't care what you wanna do. You gon' get yo' ass out here and work like the rest of these hoes. Ain't none of y'all special!" He took a step back and smacked her face, then grabbed her by the hair and pushed her toward the Navigator so hard that she crashed into it and fell to the ground.

I shook my head. Fuck that. I threw my car in park and tucked all of my money under the seat before adjusting the .38 on my waist and getting out. I jogged over to where they were and got in between them, standing face to face with the chubby nigga, while she tried to make it to her feet. "Yo, you ain't gotta be beating her like that, my nigga. That shit ain't cool," I said, already having visions of popping this stud in the stomach or something.

He frowned and stepped further into my face. "What the fuck you say, lil' nigga?" His breath smelled he'd just eaten some kind of fish. I didn't like it being blown on me. I already didn't like dudes to begin with.

I pushed him as hard as I could and watched him fly backward into her front gate. He stumbled and nearly lost his balance, and I was on his ass, grabbing him by his Versace gold and black shirt, wrapping it into my fist with my other one pulling back, ready to buss him in his shit.

Aaliyah ran over and grabbed my arm. "No, don't hit him, Rich, please. If you do, he gon' kill me later," she cried.

Now that she was standing close to me I could see what had to be his hand print on her face. That shit got me even more pissed off. I noticed that there were neighbors all around starting to come out of their houses and onto their porches.

"What? This nigga beating you like you ain't nothing and you telling me not to whoop his ass?" I asked, confused as hell.

She looked over to him and then nodded as he struggled to get away from me by trying to pry my grip from his shirt. "Please. You just don't understand. He owns me. That's just the way it is." She whimpered, and it literally broke my heart.

I looked at this fat faced, soft ass nigga and I swear I wanted to whoop this stud in front of the whole neighborhood. I didn't know what they had going on or what she meant by that, but I felt I had to listen to her.

Especially when her mother opened the door to their house and made her way down their steps with a can of St. Ides Premium in her hand. "Hey! You! You let him go right now before I stab yo' ass!" She sat the can of beer on the steps and pulled out a steak knife from her waist band, making her way toward me.

The whole time this bitch ass nigga wasn't saying shit. He had this lil' smirk on his face that made me want to get up with him even more. I started to imagine some pimp like this getting hold of one of my sisters. That shit got me vexed. As Aaliyah's mother got closer to me, I let him go and took a step back. It was then that I noticed that five more girls had gotten out of his truck and were looking at us.

Aaliyah caught her mother before she came out of the gate. "Mama, it's okay. It was just a misunderstanding," she said, holding her hands in front of her.

The yellow nigga smiled and fixed his clothes. "Yeah, mama, it was just a misunderstanding. Ain't no need to poke this clown. He was just being a good Samaritan." He laughed, looking me in the eyes before looking back at her.

I nodded. "Check this out, homey. I don't give a fuck what y'all got going on, but when you come on this block, you check that pimp shit in at the corner. Don't be beating on this female in front of her whole neighborhood. That ain't cool, and that ain't something that these other lil' females should be witnessing. You understand that?" I felt my temper getting hot, because once again, I kept imagining this nigga snatching up either Keyonna or Kesha and doing the same things to them.

Every time my mind's eye played the movie in my head it made me want to splash this fool.

He reached and grabbed a handful of Aaliyah's hair, causing her to yelp out loud with her head tilted backward. "Like this bitch said, I own her, and since I do, I'll beat this bitch where ever I want to. Now do you understand that?"

I lowered my eyes, heated. "What?" I reached under my shirt and was about to pull that .38 special out when I looked to my right and saw Andrea running down the street in just her robe and house shoes. Seeing her made he keep my pistol tucked away. Before she could get over to where we were, I simply smiled and walked to my car, got in and pulled down the street to meet her half way. That last thing I needed was for this nigga to know that she had any relation to me.

In my opinion, the niggas in Milwaukee were cowards. Most of them weren't really about that life and they were afraid to go to war with you. So, instead of doing so, they had a habit of taking their hatred for you out on a vulnerable person in your family. That shit made me sick, so instead of stopping in front of Andrea, I drove past her and all the way off of the block, then down the alley, parking my car in the back of our crib.

TRAPHOUSE KING

She came into the house about ten minutes later. I was sitting at the living room table counting stacks and taking inventory of my product. She walked in front of the table, eyeing me with anger. I could tell because her face was red.

I slapped a rubber band around one stack after the next, pretty much ignoring her until she slapped her hand on the table. "Rich! Don't you see me standing here?"

I slapped another rubber band around the fourth stack. "Yeah, I see you. So, what's good?" I grabbed the fifth one, ready to do the same thing when she frowned, pulled a chair out and sat down at the table, taking her hand and putting it on the money to stop me in my tracks. I mugged her.

"What is wrong with you? You see some pimp nigga beating his bitch and you try and break it up? For what?" She reached and grabbed a hold of my chin.

I exhaled and looked into her pretty eyes. "I didn't know that Aaliyah was selling pussy at first. I thought it was just some nigga beating on a girl that I knew from school. That's all. I wasn't about to roll past and do nothing." I moved her hand off of the money and continued to rubber band it up in stacks of one thousand.

Andrea pushed her chair back loudly, stood up and shook her head. "So, what if that was the case? So, what if she wasn't sellin' pussy and you rolled up and saw her getting her ass whooped? That's her problem, not yours. Your priorities are me and your sisters. Fuck that lil' girl. We in here living pay check to pay check, and now we ain't even got that, and you about to risk yourself to save somebody that don't matter? Really?" She asked, looking disgusted.

I put a rubber band around the seventh stack and lowered my head. I got to feeling horrible because what she

77

was getting at was making sense, even though in my heart of hearts I knew that I would never be able to sit back and watch a female get beat by a dude without doing something. I'd grown up watching my father and many other men beat my mother senseless, so it was hard for me to see what was taking place and not try and help in any way that I could.

"What if my friend never called me and told me what was going on down there, and you'd wound up beating him senseless like you almost did Maxwell? Or what if he would have shot your Captain Save a Ho ass? Then what? What would me and the girls do, Rich? Huh? Because we can't survive without you figuring the game out and mastering that shit." She exhaled loudly and walked around until she was standing in the back of my chair.

She took both of her hands and ran them down my chest, all the way until they were on my stomach muscles. Then, she leaned down and kissed my right earlobe, sticking her tongue into my ear and twirling it around, causing my whole body to tingle.

"I love you, Rich. I don't want you to care about nobody but me and your sisters. Your heart has to be cold in order for you to make it in this world, and right now, yours isn't cold enough. You gotta say fuck everybody and everything that is outside of this household. You gotta be about your bread. Fuck saving people." She kissed my cheek, ran her hand all the way down until she was squeezing my hard, throbbing dick. "This all the chips that you made today, and if so how much is it?" She asked, sucking on my neck, unfastening my belt and unbuttoning my pants before sliding her hot hand into my briefs and stroking my dick, running her thumb all over the head in a circular motion.

My breathing got heavy. I closed my eyes for a second and then opened them. "That's seven gees right there. I'mma use it to take my lil' sisters shopping and pay up the bills for the month." I groaned as she fell to her knees, licking her lips.

She looked up at me and smiled. "Aw, you think you a man now. You think you ready to pay all my bills now, huh?" She licked my head and sucked the helmet into her mouth loudly. "What about me, Rich? Huh? I might want a fit or two. Did you think about me?" She sucked my head back into her mouth and started to suck me like a porn star, making loud, nasty sounds that were driving me crazy.

I watched her face disappear into my lap again and again before she stood up, pulled her robe to the side, and lined my dick up to her sex lips.

She sat down on him with her head tilted backward. "Grab my ass, Rich, and make me fuck you on this chair, please. I love you so much, lil' daddy. Unn- a! Yes!" she moaned.

I pulled her robe all the way open and started to suck her nipples through her blouse while I held her ass and made her fuck me as if she were riding a horse. Up and down, up and down, up and down. Every time she would come downward I'd force her hips to slam into me, making sure she was taking all of my pipe. Her titties wobbled and shook inside of her blouse, and the sight of them made me bite into my lower lip and go harder, nipping at them with my teeth.

"Rich. Rich. Rich. Aww-a. Rich. I need you. I need you. Aww. Yes. Yes, lil' daddy. Yes, fuck me. Just, like that." She started to bounce up and down on me real fast. She'd stand up and sit back down, again and again. Her thick ass cheeks covered my lap. She felt hot and extremely wet.

I could hear the sounds of our sex coming from between our legs. It sounded like somebody was chewing on their bubble gum real loud. I prayed that my sisters stayed sleep and didn't just so happen to wake up and catch her and me in the act. I would have been so embarrassed. I knew that I had to hurry up because I couldn't stand for that to happen.

Andrea must've known that I was trying to get done soon because she pulled her blouse over her breasts and exposed them to me. That was all it took. Five more of her slams into me and I was cumming deep within her womb while my tongue flicked back and forth across her right nipple.

***

By the next afternoon, me and my sisters were at the Grand Avenue Mall in downtown Milwaukee. I'd taken $4,000 with me, and even though I wasn't in any position to spend that kind of money, yet I felt like I had to get them right, so I did.

I spent $2,000 on each one of them, making sure they were up to par with their underwear and everything, before I bought them five outfits and the shoes to go along with them. I wasn't really worried about me just yet. I figured I'd get myself squared away after they were good.

Once they had all of their bags in their hands and we were headed out of Macy's, Keyonna blocked my path and shook her head as the sun beamed down on to her pretty face. She smiled. "Rich, I know you weren't lying when you said that you were going to make sure that we were good soon, but I just didn't know it was going be right away. I love you so much. You're my heart." She stepped forward and wrapped her arms around me.

I rubbed her back and nodded. Then, I tilted her chin, so I could kiss her on the forehead. As soon as my lips touched her skin she closed her eyes.

Kesha stepped closer, blushing. "I wanna hug you too, Rich. Can you hug me?" She asked with her head lowered.

Keyonna took a step back, then moved to the side so I could wrap Kesha into my arms, picking her up from the ground and raining kisses across her beautiful face as she giggled.

I felt good. I felt like I was making a lil' leeway with them, but I knew there was a long road ahead. I had to get all the way on my game. I needed more money. I needed it to come faster than it was. With all of Andrea's bills being in my lap, then the cost of making sure my sisters were continuously spoiled like princesses, I needed to rake in at least $20,000 a week. I didn't know how I was going to do it. I just knew that I had to figure it out. Then, by the grace of God, that major thing happened.

HOOD RICH

Chapter 8

It was three months after I'd taken my sister's shopping. It was early August and so hot throughout the city that it felt like we were in hell. I'd made about fifty gees, yet I only had a lil' more than twenty bands put up in my mattress. I was already planning on using that scratch to cop me a kilo of cocaine, so I could really hit the game hard, when Paper sat a lick before me that I couldn't refuse.

I sat across the table from him while he ate on a bowl of cereal, shoveling spoonful's of Cookie Crisps into his mouth and chewing with his eyes closed. I sat with my .9 millimeter on the side of me and a blunt in my hand that I was just beginning to spark.

He sat the spoon on the table, took the bowl and tilted it while he drank the chocolate milk from inside of it. After he was finished he wiped his mouth and burped. "A'ight, peep. We finna hit my mother's husband's son for a few bricks of meth. This nigga holding and he gotta come off of that shit. I got some white bitches on my team that go to college that'll buy up every gram of that shit that we yank from dude ass. Not only that, but we can take the money that we make from it and cop us a few bricks of that raw and really get into the game. Shirley already got the trap doing numbers. If we can get us a few bricks we can cook that shit the right way and turn this bitch into a smoke house. That way, whenever the fiends get they checks, they wouldn't need to go no further than us. Most of them muhfuckas just be wanting to get high and find a place where they can fuck all night, and they can do that shit here, long as they pay the fee and buy up all of our dope." He stood up and popped a stick of gum into his mouth.

I took a deep pull off of my Dro blunt and inhaled before blowing it back out. "How you know how much dope this nigga got? I thought y'all didn't get along?" I asked, remembering how Paper told me that he didn't like his mother's man because she always put him before Paper. He'd told me that he and the dude had nearly gotten into a couple fist fights over his mother. Supposedly, her husband was real possessive and controlling, and Paper didn't like that.

Paper scrunched his face. "I was over there last night, and that nigga had like ten bricks on the table, and my mother didn't say shit. Then his son came over and I watched him give him five of those, but I overheard him telling him that one of them was supposed to be sold in bulk right away. I don't know if it's gone or not, but he should definitely have a four-piece left. We can rob his ass for them and get right. Fuck Jamie!" he said, referring to his mother's husband.

I knew that that meth shit was slowly starting to slide into the ghetto, and I was thinking that if we could have a trap where we sold both meth and crack then we would be rolling in the dough. My goal of twenty thousand a week wouldn't have been nothing to hit. "Paper, so what? we finna kick this nigga door in and run in there with guns blazing? I mean, if that's what we gotta do then I'm down. I just wanna make sure that it's the route you wanna take."

Paper laughed. "Nigga, it's the only way that I know, unless you got something better." He reached for the blunt and I handed it to him.

I shook my head. "N'all, it's by any means for me. If we gotta lay dude son down, long as you don't feel it'll put your mother in danger, or it'll come back on us in no way, then we gotta do what we gotta do."

***

It was a week later, and I found myself waiting in the hallway of Jay's duplex. How Paper had managed to get into his crib was beyond me, but somehow, some way, he had, and by the time I caught up with him a block away from Jay's duplex, all he did was hand me a mask, then we ran down the alley and alongside of his house until we entered into the front door that was already opened. We stepped inside and kneeled in the dark hallway. Jay stayed upstairs, so there was a flight for us to travel up, and when I was on my way up the stairs, Paper grabbed my arm and pulled me back down, almost causing me to buss my shit. I stumbled and wound up on my knee beside him, breathing hard because I was already hyped up from thinking about what we were about to do.

He leaned over so that is mask was close to my ear. "Bruh, chill. That nigga should be here in a minute. We gon' wait until he come through that door to snatch his ass up and take him upstairs. It should be sweet 'cuz that nigga ain't really 'bout that life like that." He grabbed me and gave me a half a hug, smacking me on the back a lil' bit. "We got this. Just be cool."

I nodded. "Fa show, bruh."

Though I was telling him that, my heart was beating in my chest so hard that it hurt. I was ready to get this mission over with, so I could get back and help Keyonna and Kesha with their homework. Keyonna had been asking me about it the entire day prior to this robbery, and I knew that Kesha would need help too, so I figured we all just make a night of it. Order a pizza and knock out a few assignments.

Jay's hallway was stuffy as hell. I felt my underarms getting a lil' wet. I'd made sure that I had a nice amount of Suave deodorant under each pit. My face felt itchy from the mask and I could not control my heavy breathing. I had this weird feeling deep within the pit of my gut that my life was about to change.

About ten minutes passed before I heard Jay pull up in his Cadillac Escalade, beating Cardi B's new album. His speakers were so loud that it felt like the floor beneath us was about to cave in. I got light headed when the music stopped, and I heard him climbing up the steps and onto the porch before he was jiggling his key into the lock of the duplex.

Paper stood up and pointed his pistol at the door as it slowly opened while I traveled up three steps, so I could get out of his way.

Jay pushed the door in, and as soon as he did, Paper stepped forward and yanked him into the hallway by the use of his shirt. "Get yo' bitch ass in here, nigga," he growled before closing the door by kicking it.

Jay threw his hands in the air. "What the fuck is this about, my nigga?" he asked, acting all tough and shit.

Paper didn't waste no time. He swung his pistol and smacked Jay right on the side of the face with it so hard that he knocked him into the wall. "This ain't no game. Get yo' punk ass up them stairs and take us to the dope and the money. I know you got both in this muhfucka." He pushed him until he fell by my feet.

Jay slowly gathered himself, holding his face as he made his way up the stairs, jumping a lil' bit as he passed me. I don't think he saw me at first because the hallway was so dark. I grabbed him by the back of the neck and forced him up the stairs some more.

He stopped at the upstairs door and put his key into the lock. "Man, this shit ain't cool. I know who you is cuz. I ain't stupid," he muttered, unlocking the door and pushing it in.

Paper walked up behind him and wrapped his arm around his neck. He forced his pistol into his temple, pressing so hard that it looked like it was about to break the skin. "Oh, you know who I am, huh? Then who am I?" he asked, throwing him to the floor, and aiming his Glock at him.

Jay looked up at him with eyes wide open. "Come on, man, that don't even matter. Let me just get you this shit so y'all can go on about your business." He tried to get up and Paper kicked him in the chest, forcing him to fall backward.

"Who am I? Tell me right now or I'm about to stank yo' punk ass."

I don't know what the fuck Paper was thinking but I wasn't about to let him kill dude before we got everything that we had come for. I was hoping that he wasn't all doped up on pills and shit because it seemed like whenever he was that it caused him to make some stupid decisions. I was trying to get paid, not be on some kamikaze type shit.

Jay scooted backward on his ass. "Look, Paper, it ain't that serious, my nigga." His head bumped into his entertainment system. "You ain't have to do this shit. I would've put you on. That's my word, nigga. After all, we're supposed to be step-brothers." He swallowed and lowered his eyes.

Paper cocked his Glock and took his mask off of his face. "Nigga, fuck you." He tucked the mask into his waist band, reached down and pulled Jay up. "Take me to this meth and I want all the money too or I'm killing you. I ain't my brother's keeper, nigga." He pushed Jay into the dining room so hard that he bumped into the table and knocked it over.

I got to getting nervous because I didn't know if anybody stayed downstairs or not. The last thing we needed was for the neighbors to call the police.

Jay picked the table back up and looked over his shoulder at Paper with is upper lip curled. "It's good, nigga. You can have this lil' chump change. You got me. I should've known you wasn't right." He led us into the kitchen where he kneeled and opened the cabinet below the sink. After it was opened, he stuck his head inside of it and got to pulling out all kinds of household cleaning products before we heard him beating at something.

Once again, I started to get nervous; worried about the potential downstairs neighbors. "Yo, this nigga got neighbors downstairs?" I asked, looking around the house to make sure that nobody else was there.

I had to admit that Jay's pad was laid out. It looked like everything in there was brand new and top of the line. He had mad swag. I even felt a lil' envious because we ain't have half of that shit back at Andrea's crib. I had to step my game up.

I walked back into the kitchen just as Jay started to throw one kilo after the next on to the floor. They slid for a short distance and crashed into the stove. He'd tossed out six before he pulled his head out of the cabinet. Man, I couldn't believe it because Paper had previously said that he wouldn't have more than four birds.

After he tossed out the sixth one he stood up and faced Paper. "There you go, little brother. I hope you get your money right. It ain't have to be like this though. I thought we was better than that." He wiped sweat from his forehead and looked into Paper's eyes.

I took the six birds and dumped them into the garbage can and pulled the bag out of the garbage. I didn't have nothing to do with what they had going on. "Paper, fuck what he talking about. What's good with that bread? He gotta have some money in this muhfucka somewhere."

Paper took a step back and upped his Glock, pointing it at Jay's face. "Yeah, nigga, fuck what you talking about. Where that bread at?" He turned the gun sideways for dramatic effect I guessed.

Jay covered his face and lowered his head. "Man, get off of that bullshit. I just gave you six birds, my nigga. You can't take that shit and go?" he asked, walking backward.

I frowned after I saw Paper pause as if he was thinking things over. I dropped the bag on the floor and walked over to Jay and grabbed him by the neck, putting the .38 Special under his chin. He yelped and started to shake. "Check this out, homey. You ain't no kin to me and I don't give a fuck about you one way or the other. You finna take me to this bread and we gon' leave you with your life, or you can play games and you can get yo' ass murked. Now answer my question. Paper, do this nigga got some neighbors downstairs?" I looked over my shoulder at him while forcing my gun upward into the bottom of Jay's chin.

Paper shook his head. "Not that I know of. Ask him."

Jay shook his head. "N'all man, it's vacant. And I ain't got no money in here. I'm smarter than that," he said with his head tilted backward.

I shook my head. "N'all, we ain't about to play these games. I'ma ask you one more time. Take me to the money." I flared my nostrils under my mask, feeling myself getting heated. There was no way possible I was about to leave Jay's house without at least five bands.

He kept his lips sealed, looking at me with glossy eyes. "I ain't got no money here, man. That's all there is to it. Do what you gotta do."

Before I could even stop myself, I took a step back, aimed my pistol and blew his right knee cap off. *Boom.* Fire spat out of the barrel, causing smoke to rise to the ceiling. The small kitchen lit up and there was a distinct smell of gun powder in the air.

Jay fell on to his back, holding his knee, hollering at the top of his lungs. Blood oozed from between his fingers. "Arrgh! Arrgh! Okay, muthafucka. Okay." He scooted backwards on his ass, leaving a trail of blood. Tears ran down his cheeks and it smelled like he'd shat himself. It had been the first time I had ever shot anybody, and to be honest I found myself a lil' spooked and excited at the same time.

I held on to the handle of the gun tighter, ready to pop his ass again if I had to since the damage had already been done.

Paper stepped around with his eyes bucked. "A'ight, nigga, just take me to the money before I let my shooter hit you up." He picked Jay up and wrapped his arm around his neck.

I watched them leave to the back of the house with Jay hopping on one foot. I kneeled and stuck my head back into the cabinet, trying to see where it was that Jay had gotten the birds from. Since he was acting so funny about giving us the money I figured he was one of them types that always tried to keep something tucked away, even while he was getting robbed. That made me suspicious.

It didn't take long for me to find the hole that he'd gotten the bricks from. I leaned forward and stuck my hand into it, feeling around while roaches crawled out of the wall in a frenzy. I felt downward until my hand came into contact with what felt the same material the other bricks were wrapped in. I pulled one up and looked it over, and sure enough there it was, another kilo of meth I assumed. I took the brick and threw it out of the cabinet. Then, I felt deeper into the hole and was able to toss out another four bricks before I felt around and saw that there were no more. I crawled backward and stood up. I took my shirt and popped it out. Three big ass roaches fell off of me and scattered to their escape. I grabbed the four bricks and tossed them in the bag before running to the back of the house where Paper and Jay was.

I got there just in time to see Jay placing a bundle of cash into a pillow case. He was laying on his side with his safe open in front of him, filling up the pillowcase while Paper held his pistol on him.

"Hurry up nigga." Paper growled.

Blood gushed out of Jay's knees. The hole looked like it had gotten bigger. I could smell clearly now that he'd shat himself.

He tossed in the last bundle and handed the pillowcase to Paper. It looked chunky. "Here, man. It's all in there. Now can one of y'all please drive me to the hospital?" He groaned, out of breath.

Paper tied the pillowcase in a knot and tossed it to me. "Hold this, bruh, and go open the backdoor." He cocked the hammer of his pistol and lowered it to Jay's face.

I grabbed the money and shrugged. I knew what Paper was about to do and I guess I had to make peace with that. It was the life that we were in. After all, Jay knew who he was and that would've never worked. So, I took everything and opened the backdoor just like he asked me to. As soon as I pulled the door open, I heard the shots.

Boom. Boom. Boom.

Paper was running toward me and we hit it down the back stairs to the backyard and down the alley, running as fast as we could until we made it back to my car.

That night, Paper and I counted out $100,000 and separated the ten kilos of dope. The last four that I had pulled out of the wall were not meth. They turned out to be pure Colombian cocaine. So pure that the coke looked as if it had a light pink tinge to it. The only thing I could think of was that we were about to get money.

Chapter 9

Four months later, and in the month of December, me and Paper had the trap rocking so hard that it was normal for us to have a line of addicts in the backyard waiting for us to serve them. On top of that, we'd turn Paper's trap into a straight smoke house, where we allowed for fiends to come inside and smoke until they ran out of money. In addition to that, they were able to mingle and fuck the other hypes as long as one of the two of them were still buying our product. I made sure that we supplied everything too. I had bags of glass pipes and chars that were basically scrubbing brillo pads. I had lighters, alcohol pads and even ashtrays. Plus, I kept something booming out of the speakers from the old school, so the fiends could relax and take a load. Shit, we even supplied them with condoms when it was time for them to do the do.

The money was coming fast, and it was plentiful. I got into this phase where I was barely spending anything on myself because I felt like my sisters had been deprived of so much, so I took to spoiling them and making sure that they had the absolute best of the best. Every weekend I'd make sure that I took them on shopping sprees where I'd spend about three gees apiece on each of them. Keyonna took a major liking to everything Prada and Christian Louboutin, while Kesha was crazy over Gucci and Steve Madden. Neither one of their tastes bothered me. I just wanted to make sure that they were happy and kept money on their debit cards.

Keyonna turned eighteen the following Spring, and months prior to her eighteenth birthday she kept on begging me to buy her a Jeep. She'd already gotten her driver's license and maintained a 3.5 grade point average that made me proud. So, while I already knew that I was going to get her whatever she wanted, I made it seem like buying her a Jeep was out of the question. For about three weeks before her birthday all she did was mope around the house with a long face. She refused to give me her normal hugs and kisses and did all that she could to avoid me. It literally killed me to endure those three weeks because I missed her displays of affection. Keyonna was my first sister and the first person in this world I'd learned to protect even before myself. Our bond was strong, and for three weeks it seemed nonexistent and that crushed me, to say the least.

On the morning of her birthday, I woke her up with a big smile on my face, after pulling her sleeping mask from her eyes. "Get up, baby sister, it's your birthday and I want you to roll with me today. Here." I handed her a small bag from Zale's. "Open it." I leaned forward and kissed her on the forehead. "Happy birthday."

She sat all the way up and pulled down her Prada duvet, wiping the cold out of her eyes. "Thank you, Rich, but I'm still mad at you," she said looking into my eyes with her twin-like hazel ones. She sat the bag on her lap and crossed her arms.

I frowned. "Dang, you ain't even gon' look and see what I bought you?" I asked, feeling some type of way.

Kesha came into the room with her toothbrush inside of her mouth. She took it out for a second. "She still made because she wanted a Jeep for her birthday and she overheard you telling Andrea that you couldn't afford one this year, but that you'd make sure that she was good for her nineteenth birthday." She stuck her toothbrush back into her mouth and allowed it to do its job.

Keyonna rolled her eyes. "So, what Kesha? Damn, you always gotta run your big mouth. Ain't nobody said nothing to you, and you're damn right I'm mad. A girl only turns eighteen one time. My sixteenth birthday sucked. I didn't even have a cake. Now I have to wait all the way until my nineteenth one to be happy. It's just not fair. It isn't." She lowered her face into her hands and started to sob loudly, shaking her head.

Kesha shook her head and removed her electric toothbrush once again. "You got that girl spoiled, Rich. For real, she's way too soft and thinks she's supposed to get everything that she wants." She sucked her teeth. "Keyonna, if you weren't so damn spoiled you'd look in the bag and find the keys to your Jeep that you don't deserve, freaking diva. Its parked in the front of the house, if you must know." Kesha walked out of the room with her toothbrush whirring inside of her mouth.

Keyonna took her hands away from her face. Her eyes were bugged out of her head. "What? Is she serious?" she asked, coming to her knees in the bed, grabbing the bag and reaching inside of it before throwing all of the jewelry boxes to the side and pulling out the Mercedes Benz's keys. "Oh my God! You didn't Rich! I know you didn't buy me what I wanted for my birthday!" She jumped out of the bed and hugged me briefly before running out of her room and to the front window where she pulled the curtain back and screamed so loud that it hurt my ears. "Ahh!" She unlocked the front door and pulled it open, running down the stairs and into the sunlight. She stopped in front of the pink 2019 Benz truck that was laced with the black and pink Faccio rims that had Prada's logo all over them. She looked over her shoulder at me and dropped to her knees, crying into her hands again.

I walked over to her and pulled her up, wrapping my arms around her small waist, hugging her to my body. "Never doubt me, lil' sis. I love you way too much to ever let you down. I know you had a rough first sixteen years in life, but I promise to make the rest better from here on out." I kissed her forehead while she sobbed underneath me. "Let's go take it for a spin."

She shook her head. "I love you so much, Rich. I swear with everything that I am. I love you with all of me." She hugged me tightly then popped the doors of her truck by use of the remote on her key chain. I watched her open the driver's door and get behind the wheel. She looked all around the truck, crying, then put the key into the ignition and turned it on. "Come on, Rich. I want to take my first drive inside of it with you!" she hollered, and I almost melted.

I jumped inside, and she pulled away from the curb.

***

Later that day, I felt that Kesha was feeling some type of way, because after me and Keyonna got back, she seemed to be more quiet than usual. So, I asked her if she would take a ride with me and she agreed to. As I pulled from in front of the house I turned to her and asked her what was good.

She took a tuft of her long, curly hair and placed it behind her ear. She looked so much like my mother that at times it scared me. "Rich, at times, I feel like you love Keyonna more than you do me, and I hate feeling that way because you two are all that I have. I mean, besides Andrea." She swallowed and looked over at me, pursing her lips. Doing so caused her deep dimples to appear on each cheek.

I felt like I'd been punched in the stomach by a heavy-weight boxer or something. "What makes you feel like that, Kesha, when you should know that it isn't the case? I love the both of my princesses the same." I reached and turned on the air conditioner and adjusted one of the vents so some of the air blew directly onto me. I felt real hot all of the sudden.

Kesha shrugged her. "I don't know. I guess I just feel like you make more of a fuss over her than you do me. Then, she's always all under you and you guys spend more time together than we do. And for my birthday last month you got me some pretty nice things, but it wasn't a truck. That's huge." She exhaled. "I guess I understand a little bit. I mean, she is more beautiful than I am, and I'm more of a tom boy, real quiet and stuff. You probably relate more to her being a sister than you do me." She was quiet for a moment before looking out of my passenger's window.

I must've been quiet for a full two minutes. I was shocked and didn't know what to say. I started to replay me and Keyonna's relationship over in my mind, then compared it to the one I had with Kesha. I was less than halfway started before I confirmed that she was right. I favored Keyonna more than I did her and I didn't even realize it. "Damn, I'm so sorry, Kesha. I didn't even realize what I've been doing. I need you to know that I love you just as much. You're my heart, lil' sister, and I'm going to get better at splitting my love and time down the middle between the two of you because you should never feel left out. You hear me?"

She nodded and then blinked. Tears fell down her cheeks, then she was crying full on. "I miss our mother so much, Rich. I don't think I can go through this life without her. I feel so lost and so unloved. She was our rock. Now what do we have? I'll never be pretty enough to have anybody love me as much as she did." She covered her face again and broke into a fit of tears.

I pulled up to a stop sign and threw my car in park, leaned over and pulled Kesha to me, rubbing the back of her head while she cried into my chest. "Baby, it's going to be okay. I love you just as much as mama did, and you're one of the most beautiful women ever created. You are an angel— perfect in every single way. Never forget that. Do you hear me?"

She nodded once again while she cried harder into my chest.

I don't know why or how I wound up at my mother's grave, but somehow, some way, me and Kesha wound up there with her standing in front of me with my arms wrapped around her frame and my chin on her shoulder, kissing her soft cheek every so often.

Prior to us standing and overlooking her grave, I'd watched Kesha lay a golden rose on top of the grave and kiss her head stone. "We have to be something, Rich. We have to find a way to make our mother proud. She battled so many demons and was unable to give us the life that she wanted to because of them, so it's for us to make it happen. It's why I'm going to be a doctor. I want to save those that can't save themselves."

I held her tighter and kissed her cheek again. I loved my lil' sister so much. "Kesha, I'm gon' make sure that you're able to be anything that you want to. All you have to do is the schoolwork and I'll take care of everything else, I promise."

She looked up at me and smiled. "I believe you too, Rich. I know you got me. I just get jealous sometimes because Keyonna is so forward and she isn't so afraid of you rejecting her when I am. Every time you say no to me it makes me feel so alone. I wish I had her moxie." She exhaled loudly.

I laughed because I knew what my sister was getting at, even though she was afraid to say it. An hour later we pulled up at the Mercedes Benz lot, and three hours after all of the paperwork was finished, she was able to drive off of the lot in her own Mercedes Benz coupe. It was a good thing that I was cool with the owner, and that he dabbled with that meth from time to time because I didn't have a problem with him taking all cash, even though it proceeded ten thousand, when usually they'd flag the money and call the authorities. But this day turned out to be a good one. I was able to make both of my sisters happy, and that in turn made me happy.

***

Later that night, at about two in the morning, I was rolling from Paper's house on my way back to Andrea's when I rolled past the alley that came right before I entered onto our block and saw Aaliyah running out of it with blood all over the front of her short, Burberry dress. She was looking over her shoulder before she fell onto her knees and got back up, running full speed with something in her hand.

I slammed on the brakes and threw my car in reverse, pulling backward until I was in front of her. "Aaliyah! Aaliyah!" I hollered but figured she couldn't hear me because of my passenger's window being rolled up.

She was still running, looking backward.

Finally, I got out of the car. "Aaliyah!"

She froze in place and screamed out loud before looking forward and seeing that it was me. She shook her head. "Help me, Rich! Help, please! I swear I didn't mean to!" she hollered, looking as if she were about to have a nervous breakdown.

I waved her over. "Come on, man, you good. Hurry up."

She looked down the alley again, then ran over to my car and waited for me to open the passenger's door for her.

Chapter 10

I swallowed hard as the rain began to pour with thunder roaring in the sky. Within seconds I was drenched as Aaliyah stuck her head out of my car with tears running down her face.

"Is she dead, Rich? Please tell me she me isn't." She cried.

Now the rain began to come down so hard that it was difficult for me to see in front of me. My clothes were matted to my skin and my socks felt like they were filled with water. The Air Max did very little to shield me from the elements. I reached my hand out and placed two fingers to the light skinned woman's neck and waited to see if I felt a pulse. Her midsection was bloodied. Aaliyah had already admitted to me that she stabbed the woman three times in the stomach after they'd fought there in the alley behind our houses.

I shook my head and looked over my shoulder at her. "She gone, Aaliyah." I stood up and jogged to the car. "What you want me to do?" I asked, not really seeing a solution. Old girl was dead. The only thing we could do was leave her right there in the alley and allow for somebody to stumble across her the next day and call the police.

Aaliyah's eyes were wide open in fear. "She's dead? Aw shit. He gon' kill me too. That was his bottom bitch. She was showing me the ropes. He gon' know that I did it. What am I supposed to do?" She whimpered.

I took a deep breath and looked her over closely, noticing how bad she was shaking. I understood that she was incredibly afraid of this dude and I still didn't even know his name. I jogged around the car and got into the driver's seat, closing my door, taking time out to gather my thoughts before turning to her like two minutes later. "Look, Aaliyah, ain't nothing we can do about that because ol' girl dead. We just gotta get away from this area and see what happens. I'mma put you up in a motel until we can get some things figured out, okay?" I reached over and pulled her wet hair off of her cheek.

She shook her head. "I ain't got no money for a hotel. I wasn't even out here that long before all this stuff happened. She started to smack me around right away, like she couldn't wait for Ken to drop us off. I don't think she liked me," she said, looking into her lap and shaking her head.

I threw my car in drive and pulled off. "Don't worry about it because we ain't taking you to no hotel. I'mma put you up in this motel over on twenty-fifth and Wisconsin Street. They only charge about forty dollars a night. I'mma book you for a full week so you can gather yourself."

She sat back in her seat and looked out of the window. "Thank you, Rich. I swear I'mma pay you back, somehow, some way."

* * *

Aaliyah came out of the bathroom of the Super Eight Motel with a small bottle of Patron. She took it and placed it to her lips, swallowing it in large gulps before plopping down on the bed and running her fingers through her hair. "I don't know what I'm going to do."

I sat my phone on the night stand after texting Andrea that I'd be home in like an hour. I told her I had some business to handle and then I would be on my way. After that was done, I got up and sat on the bed next to Aaliyah, just as the first tears began to slide down her cheeks. I placed my arm around her shoulder and pulled her to me. "Aaliyah, its gon' be alright. I ain't about to let nothing happen to you. You gotta trust me on that. Now, I don't really know how that fool Ken get down, but I ain't feeling him already. I know you got a good explanation for murking ol' girl in that alley, so let me know what's good and we can go from there."

She nodded, then wiggled her shoulders, coming from out of my embrace and standing up to pace the floor. "Meeka hated me ever since Ken brought me into his stable." She exhaled loudly. "Rich, I don't want you judging me and shit after I tell you a few things, and I don't need your sympathy either. I been figuring things out on my own ever since I was sixteen years old. Ain't nobody ever did nothing for me, that's the first thing you gotta understand. You feel me?" She looked up and into my hazel eyes.

I got up and sat on the chair by the door, nodding. "Yeah, I feel you, and I need you to know that I'd never judge you. I always liked you, Aaliyah, ever since we were in school. To be honest I was kind of wondering how it was that you'd went from being a good girl to selling pussy for this Ken nigga. I hope I ain't overstepping my bounds in saying that."

She looked at me for a few seconds with a blank stare on her face and then laughed. "Yeah, you are, but it's good. I mean, after seeing what I just did, ain't no reason for me to keep a secret from you." Her chest rose and then she blew out the air, shaking her head with her eyes closed. "I been through so much, Rich." She raised her head and looked me in the eyes. "I ain't ever had the opportunity to be a good girl. From as far back as I could remember, my mother has always used me as a tool to get the drugs that she needed to fulfill her habit. My father died when I was only four years old from an overdose of heroin. But even when he was alive, all he did was beat me and my mother and make our lives a living hell. In fact, he's the one that turned her out on to the dope. My life has sucked ever since then."

I nodded. "My pops turned my mother out too, and as crazy as it sounds, my mother overdosed off of that drug, so I guess you can say that we got a few things in common. Not to interrupt you or nothin'."

She shook her head. "N'all, it's good. I guess I needed to hear something like that to give me strength to tell you my own story. Did your mother pass away like my father did?"

I nodded. "She passed away on March 21st, of 2018."

She swallowed. "I'm sorry to hear that." She exhaled. "Well, ever since my mother put that needle in her veins she's been dead too. I don't think I've gone more than two days in a row without her beating me or scamming me out of something. Back when you saw me in school, I had so much going on inside of me that every single day I contemplated suicide. The reason I worked so hard in school was because I felt it was my only way of escaping the ghetto and her, but then she wound up falling so far into debt because of her heroin usage that she wound up selling me to Ken six months after I turned eighteen. Do you know that I have four scholarships to attend universities down south, Clark being one of them, which was my first choice, and I can't even go, even though I'm being offered a full ride on an athletic scholarship to run track, because I am a slave to Ken?" She shook her head. "My life sucks, Rich."

I stood up with the intentions to walk over so I could console her, but she held up a hand, stopping me in my tracks. That made me sit back down. "Just tell me what happened tonight, and we can move forward from there." My phone vibrated. I picked it up and looked at the face. It was a text from Andrea saying that she needed me home now. That her body was calling for mine. I smiled and started to imagine some of the things that we were about to get into before I snapped back into reality.

"Probably one of your lil' chicks wondering where you are, huh?" she asked with her head down again.

I nodded. "Yeah, but it's okay. I'm here with you right now, and I wanna make sure you're okay before I go anywhere. You matter to me, regardless to what you may think. I'mma help you get out of this situation."

She pursued her lips and started to pace again. "Meeka waited until Ken let us out of his truck before she got to pushing me and telling me that if I didn't listen that she was going to kick my ass. She had already told me time and time again that she didn't like me because she felt that I thought I was too good to sell pussy, even though I never said I was." She stopped in her tracks, seemingly as if she was lost in time before she came back to. "Anyway, so there were these two older white men that pulled up on us while we were walking down Lisbon, and I guess they wanted to pick us up so we could screw each other in front of them before they fucked us, but it's like I was trying to tell her before, I'm on my cycle, so I'm not screwing nobody because doing it while I'm on, that is just nasty to me. Well this girl takes it upon herself to tell the men that I was on my cycle and asked them if that would be a problem. Well, I guess that was appealing to them because the next thing I knew, Meeka walked away from the car and over to me saying that they were willing to give us five hundred dollars apiece if they could fuck me bare back without a rubber, and I snapped on her ass right in front of them, so much so that it caused them to drive away." She exhaled loudly.

"That pissed her off because the next thing I knew, she had a handful of my hair, pulling me into the alley like I was her child or something. I waited until we were half way inside of the alley before I pulled the small steak knife out of its sheath and threatened to stab her with it. She must've thought that I was playing because she rushed me in an attacking fashion and I stabbed her three times until she fell to her knees. That's when you saw me running out of the alley, and the rest is history." She sat on the edge of the bed with her head down before looking over to me. "I ain't ever screwed nobody without a rubber. I'm terrified of diseases and I get myself checked once a month. When Meeka tried to force me to play Russian Roulette with my life, something in me just snapped and I couldn't take it anymore." She licked her lips and looked off into space. "So, how are you going to help me?"

I swallowed and got up just to walk over and kneel by her side. "I'll help you in any way that you need me to. All you gotta tell me is what you really need from me and I got you. That's my word."

She shrugged. "I know Ken gon' be looking for me. I need to find a way to get rid of him because if he catches me he's going to kill me. I know that for a fact. Since I been working for him, I've witnessed him kill two of the girls by choking them to death. He doesn't play and has already sent ten text messages asking where I am. It's a guaranteed ass whoopin' if he texts you twice with no response, so I'm terrified."

I didn't like this Ken nigga. He seemed like a bully of women to me, and I hated every man that felt like he had to fuck over a female just to feel as if he was more than what he was. I knew I could handle dude for her. "Check this out, Aaliyah. I want you to chill here and just relax for about a week until things calm down out there. In the meantime, I'll make sure you're good, and anything you need all you'll have to do is hit me up and I'm gon' bring it to you."

"But what about Ken? Rich, I'm telling you that dude ain't gon' rest until he finds me, and when he does, he's going to kill me. I can't run from him for forever. So, what do I do?" she asked, getting up and walking away from me. She picked up her purse and pulled out the steak knife that was encased in a leather sheath. Before she pulled it out of the sheath, I could see that it was drenched in dried up, burgundy blood. She pulled out the blade and looked down at it. "I'm not gon' let him do me like he did those other girls, Rich. I'm not going to be his victim. I've been everybody's victim for way too long. I can't take it anymore. You have to help me." She turned the knife over in her hand, looking at it as if she were in a trance.

I got to my feet, walked into the bathroom, took one of the white towels and came back out of it. "Aaliyah, I gotta get rid of that knife for you. If the police find that with Meeka's DNA on it, they gon' lock you away for a long time. Then, there will be more things that you'll have to worry about that are worse than Ken." I reached out with the towel. "Give it to me."

She looked down at it for a long time then placed it inside of the sheath and laid it on the towel before sitting on the bed. "I can't believe that I messed my life up like this. All in one night. I don't know what to do." She shook her head and lowered it with her shoulders slouched.

"Like I said, you just chill here for a week or so. I'll keep checking in on you, and within that length of time we'll figure out what we're going to do with dude. But I don't want you worrying about nothing. I know it's real hard to trust anyone other than yourself, but this one time you're going to have to go out on a limb. I got you." I stood up and pulled her into my arms, wrapping them around her and holding her tightly. I stroked her hair to try and make her feel comfortable. I didn't understand why I cared about her situation so much, but there was just something in me that was drawn to Aaliyah, and I knew that I had to help her, no matter what it would wind up costing me in the long run.

**

We exchanged numbers after I got back from a restaurant called John Red Hots. I thought it'd be cool to snatch her up a Gyro dinner with chili-cheese fries and a Sprite soda. I had to put something on her stomach. I was worried that she was going to fall into a worrying type of depression that caused for a person to go without food for a lengthy time. I knew that couldn't be healthy, so I tried to nip that in the bud right away. It took a lil' coaxing before she took her first bite, but after it was in her mouth, she was good to go.

I took the murder weapon and broke it down into three pieces after soaking it in bleach and rubbing alcohol at the motel, before wiping it clean and throwing it piece by piece into the Wisconsin River that night. I didn't want to see her lose her life over protecting herself. I felt like she still had so much life to live and that all she needed was for somebody to love and care about her. I didn't see any problem with that person being me.

***

Andrea woke me up at six the next morning by jumping on the bed and straddling me. She leaned down and sucked all over my neck before trailing her kisses all the way down my body, until she was at my boxers. There, she reached inside of them and pulled out my pipe, stroking it up and down before sucking it into her mouth, spearing her head back and forth on my meat, causing my toes to curl. I spread my legs and looked down on her with my eyes lowered, threatening to roll into the back of my head.

She sucked harder and harder, stopped and popped it out of her mouth, allowing for it to rest up against her cheek. "Rich, wake up. Wake up, baby, because I found a concoction that's about to make us rich. You gotta see this shit," she said, before sucking me back into her mouth and really going to town on me.

I groaned and humped into her. My eyes rolled into the back of my head. My abs tightened. I reached down and grabbed a hand full of her hair, gripping her curls, forcing her to take more and more of me. The more I forced her to inhale, the harder she sucked, moaning around my dick and licking all over the head. Then, she stopped once again and slid up my body, reached under herself and lined me up before sliding down my pole, taking me deeply into her hot womb that felt a hundred degrees hotter than her mouth.

She placed her hands on my chest and started to twerk on my dick, fucking me like a prized cowgirl. Her hips popped forward and then jerked backward, riding me fast and hard while the headboard slammed into the wall loudly.

"Uh, uh, uh, uh, uh, umm-a, ooo-ah! Yes, Rich, um, yes, yes, daddy. It. Feel. So. Good. It feel. So good-a!" She moaned loudly, bouncing up and down on me like crazy.

I held her hips and directed my pipe to keep hitting her G spot. Her titties bounced up and down inside of her tight tank top, threatening to come out of it. I reached up and grabbed ahold of them. Pulling the nipples through the fabric, I made them stand up a cool inch while she rode me, looking into my hazel eyes. Her womb was sucking at me like a wet, hot vacuum cleaner.

I sat up and flipped her over onto her stomach, causing her to scream out loud. "Ahh! Fuck, Rich! What are you finna do to me?" she asked, coming to all fours and laying her face on the bed, looking back at me in want, need and desire. "I need you, Rich. I need you to fuck me hard for figuring things out for us. We finna be paid, daddy. Watch." She spread her ass cheeks apart and licked her lips.

I still didn't know what she was talking about, and even though I wanted to know, I felt like it could wait. I was looking at the crinkle of her plump ass and I wanted to hit that muhfucka. The way she was holding it open, it let me know that she wanted me to hit it too. So, I leaned forward and licked up and down and in between her ass cheeks. My tongue slid in and out of her anus to taste what I was about to be hitting. My dick was throbbing against my belly.

"Unnn-a, Rich! Yes. Eat that ass, baby. Eat it, then fuck me with that big ass dick. Please, daddy. Uhhh! Shit, Rich. Now! Please, now." She moaned, spreading her cheeks wider.

I was already stroking my dick with the strawberry KY jelly, getting it ready before I placed the head on her hole and eased my way inside of her backdoor. Grabbing her hips, I was going to town like a savage. *Bam, bam, bam,*

bam, bam, bam, bam, bam! was the sound my stomach made as it slammed into her soft ass cheeks.

"Rich, Rich, wait, daddy. Wait, ooh, ooh, ooh, yes, yes, fuck me, daddy. Fuck me. Uhhh-a, you killing me. Uhh! It. Feel. So. Uhhh-a!" She screamed.

I noticed that she was under her belly pinching her clitoris and rubbing it in a circle while I pounded into that ass, loving the feel of the tightness. I knew I couldn't hold back that much longer, so I sped up the pace and went animal status on her until I felt myself cumming deep within her body while she slammed back into me and moaned at the top of her lungs.

***

Two hours later, after our shower, I sat at the dining room table in my boxers and wife beater while Andrea stood before me with a mask over her face, pouring about seven grams of dope onto a small plate and sifting through it with a razor blade.

"I knew I could figure out the right ingredients to make this shit a success, and now that I have, this dope will be able to keep them fiends high for at least four hours at a time and be twice as addicting," she said, pulling her mask down, and allowing for it to hang around her neck. She smiled and nodded while biting into her bottom lip.

I looked down at the cocaine. It looked as if it were shining almost like a diamond. I pulled the plate closer to me and took the razor blade out of her hand, sifting through it. "So, you mean to tell me that this coke is mixed with meth, and with the way you blended the two, they're going to work cohesively and fuck our feigns for the greater good of our pockets?" I scrunched my face and continued to look the product over.

She laughed and smiled, taking the plate away from me. "All I did was cut the seven grams of cocaine with a gram of meth and cleaned it up a lil' bit with this B12 and Sudafed tablets. That concoction is what you're looking at, and it's going to make us rich. Mark my words on that. I'mma spend the day cooking up a half of kilo while the girls are at school. I want you to take the fourteen grams that I already got ready for you to the trap and have one of your customers try this shit out. Let me know what's good and we'll go from there." She licked her juicy lips. "I ain't new to this shit, Rich. I been around nothin' but hustlers my whole life. I know how to get us to where we need to go. All you gotta do is keep on handling your end of things and I'll get us right. Okay, baby?"

I smiled and nodded. "Yeah, okay."

She came around, leaned down and kissed me on the lips, sucking allover them before walking away with her Fendi skirt hugging her ass like a second skin. I couldn't do nothing but shake my head as I felt myself getting aroused all over again.

Forty-five minutes later, I snatched up the half ounce of mixture that Andrea had put together, stuffed it deep into my underwear, grabbed my pistol amongst other things, jumped in my whip and headed to Paper's trap. As I opened the door to Andrea's house and stepped outside, I saw that the block was flooded with police officers and cars. They had one of the corners blocked off because so many of their cars were in the middle of the street. They looked as if they were having some kind of a meeting. This was the next day after Meeka had been killed, so I figured that they were out to investigate her murder since it happened one alley over.

I came down the stairs and hurried to my whip, looking down the street one time and saw that there was yellow tape around the front of Aaliyah's mother's house. There were also police in her yard as well. I wanted to do my own investigation, but I already knew that it would have been idiotic, so I jumped into my whip and pulled off of the block, driving as carefully as I could because I couldn't stand for one of those pigs to mess with me.

I got to Paper's crib safe and sound, just as the sun came from behind the clouds with a vengeance. He opened the door with a big blunt in his mouth and a stressed look written across his face.

I stepped in past him and waited for him to close the door. "What's good, bruh?"

Shirley came from the back of the house with just a t-shirt on and a cigarette in her hand, nearly gone. She came over to me and I gave her a quick hug before stepping back. She had this thing where every time I hugged her, she took it upon herself to grope my ass, and I wasn't feeling that shit, but I didn't want to hurt her feelings. So, I let her hug me but always tried to keep it short and sweet, so she couldn't get so comfortable that it would cause her to do none of that dumb shit.

"Hey, nephew, I was hoping you showed up. Did Paper tell you that I'm throwing a smoker's party here for my birthday?" she asked, taking the cigarette and dumping the ashes into an ashtray.

I shook my head. "N'all, I just got here, but I'm sure the homey gon' let me know what's good when he get the chance."

Shirley shook her head. "Well, we just getting our taxes, and even though I didn't work that much last year, I did for about six months, so I should get back a nice chunk of change. I got twenty of my closest friends and we wanna take my birthday and make a weekend of it, but Paper say he gotta get your approval."

Paper frowned. "Damn, Shirley, let me holler at my nigga. I got this shit. I don't need your help," he said, trying to push her out of the living room.

She swatted at his hands. "Let me go, boy. You ain't gotta push me. I can walk on my own." She turned around to look over his shoulder at me. "It's gon' be some nice money in it for y'all, Rich. Especially if y'all pushing that cheesy dope."

As soon as she said that, something clicked in my brain as I watched Paper pick her skinny-self up, getting ready to carry her to the back of the house. I stopped him. "Wait a minute, bruh, I need to let her test something for me. It's important."

Paper sucked his teeth. "Nigga, I gotta holler at you on some real shit. Can't that wait?" he asked, looking irritated.

I shook my head. "Hell n'all. Especially if she talking about throwing a smoker's party here for her birthday. I need for her to test this new product out and tell me what she thinks." I pulled the half ounce out of my crotch and sat on the couch, taking the mirror that was on the table with crack residue already on it, and breaking off a chunk of Andrea's mixture before handing about a dime bag's worth to Shirley.

She held out her hand and I dropped it inside of it. She picked up the crystal rock and looked it over closely. "I can already tell that I ain't gon' like this, because it don't look right. I like for my dope to have a yellow tinge to it. This shit right here look like something else." She pulled her pipe out of her dirty bra and licked her crusty lips, getting ready to sit on the couch before Paper interrupted her.

He shook his head. "Un-un, Shirley. Go smoke that shit in there and let us know what's good when you done. For now, I gotta holler at my mans on some important shit. A'ight?"

She rolled her eyes and stood all the way up. "You sho' be acting funny when Rich come around. But when it's just me and you in here, you're the nicest muthafucka in the world. Ugh, sometimes I can't stand you, nephew." She rolled her eyes again and left out of the living room.

Paper waved her off and pulled my arm until we were both sitting on the couch. "Look, bruh, we might gotta handle my mother's husband because I think he suspicious about his son's death. He keeps asking me all these weird ass questions that's making me uncomfortable." Paper took a pull off of his blunt and handed it to me.

I took three puffs off of it and inhaled deeply before blowing it back out, wanting to slap myself across the face because I'd somewhat forgot all about the Jay situation. I handed him back the blunt. "What you think he trying to say in so many words? That you had something to do with it?" I asked as somebody started knocking on the backdoor.

Paper got up and held up a finger. "Hold on, bruh. I'll be back. It's probably just a few addicts. You want some of the money?" he asked, pulling a Ziploc bag from under the couch.

I shook my head. "I'm good, bruh. Just hurry up and let me know what you thinking so we can figure this thing out." I watched him leave into the back of the house.

My mind was spinning. I was hoping that we didn't have to kill Jamie because that would have been two murders that were up in the air that me and Paper had done, not to mention the one I was helping Aaliyah shake. I wasn't trying to be in prison for the rest of my life.

In Wisconsin, they were slaying niggas for the pettiest of crimes. I could only imagine what they would do for two homicides, but at the same time, I wasn't trying to have that fool Jamie go to them people on us either. All it'd take would be for them to start to investigate us from a distance and we'd be done. Just thinking about it was giving me the hee-bee gee-bees.

Before Paper was able to come back and sit on the couch, he'd have to answer the backdoor ten times from fiends wanting product. The trap was jumping, and it was only the beginning.

Finally, he came and sat down. "Alright, so I can kind of tell that he suspects that I had something to do with it because he can't look me in the eyes, and all yesterday when I was over my mother's house, he kept saying shit like, 'You was the only other person that knew about that shipment, Demetrius. You sho' you ain't got nothing that you want to tell me about my son's murder?' That shit had the hairs on my arms standing up on end. Then, my mother pulled me aside and asked me if I had something to do with it too, so I can tell that her nigga been all up in her head. Long story short, I wanna kill this nigga and get him out the way, as soon as possible. I just need to know if you gon' rollout with me."

Somebody started to beat on the backdoor again. He jumped up and held up another finger before disappearing into the back of the house.

The next thing I knew, Shirley came into the living room with her eyes wide open and glossy. Her lips were folded over her teeth and her hand was in her panties. She walked toward me with a delirious look on her face. "Rich, this shit good." She folded her lips back over her teeth again, then smacked her lips together loudly. "I need you and Paper to fuck me. I'm so horny. Y'all just touch all over me, baby, right now. Please, Sugars." She took her shirt and pulled it over her head, exposing her A-cup, saggy breasts that wouldn't have looked so bad had I not known the woman that they were attached too. She ran her hand back and forth inside of her black panties, closing her eyes, then opening them wide. "Please, Rich."

I stood up and held my hands out to keep her at arm's length. My nose was scrunched, and I felt sick to my stomach. I wasn't about to touch her, even with another nigga's dick. "Yo, chill with all that, Shirley. You know I got way more respect for you than that. You're like my aunty. Let's keep everything on the up and up," I said, looking over her shoulder for Paper.

She shook her head, took a step back and pulled her panties off of her ashy ankles. She threw them against the wall, laid on her back and opened her thighs wide, separating her sex lips. "Just put it in me for a little while, Rich. I'm hot down there. I need some dick. One of y'all gotta fuck me." She slid two fingers into herself and started to move them in and out, and that's when I stepped over her, just as Paper came into the living room.

"Shirley, what the fuck are you doing in here?" he asked with a handful of money. He stuffed it into his pocket, reached down and pulled her up by her kinky afro. "Get yo' ass up and get dressed." He ordered.

Shirley shook her head, ran her tongue across her lips and moaned into his face. "Fuck me, Paper! Please. I need it so bad. That shit that Rich just gave me fucking with my pussy. It's so hot in there, baby. Feel it." She reached for his hand.

He allowed for her to grab it and put in on to her sex lips before he jerked his hand away, looking at me as if he was embarrassed. "Quit that shit, Shirley! Ain't nobody on that right now. We got business to take care of! Take yo' ass in the other room. Now!" He pointed in the direction he needed for her to go.

Once again, she shook her head, dropped to the floor and opened her legs wide. "Fuck me, Paper. You know I got some good pussy. Don't be acting all like that now in front of Rich. Tell him how I get down when he ain't here." She moaned.

I bucked my eyes and couldn't believe what I was hearing, and I knew that it had some truth to it because my homey Paper was a dark-skinned nigga, but after she said what she said, he turned beet red. I was embarrassed for him.

Paper shook his head, snatched her up and carried her out of the room with her legs wrapped around him. "I'll be right back, bruh. Let me handle this bitch real quick." He carried her into the back room and closed the door.

I heard a loud slap followed by a big bang as if somebody fell to the floor. I was about to rush back there to get him off of her because I assumed that he was beating her ass, but then I heard something that blew my mind as I stood outside of the door, getting ready to turn the knob.

"You want this dick, Shirley, huh? You want me to beat this shit up? Well take this dick then, bitch. I'm finna fuck the shit out you."

I took a step back as Shirley begin to encourage him. "Fuck me, fuck me, fuck me, ooh, fuck me! Aww, aww, aww, Paper, aww, aww, oooh, fuck me, baby!"

Chapter 11

Later that night, after me and Paper got an understanding that we were going to have to take Jamie out of the game, I got a text from Aaliyah saying that she needed to see me as soon as possible. So, I confirmed with Shirley that Andrea's mixture was five times better than the cheesed version of our crack. She said not only was it better, but it made her feel like she was getting high for the first time all over again. It made her feel highly sexual and as free as a bird. She said that she would get the word out and make sure that the whole city knew that me and Paper were holding the number one product in town. Her birthday party was in two days and I figured that it'd be the perfect time to get our dope into the hands of as many fiends as possible. I was ready to blow up and to get as much money as possible.

When I got to the motel, Aaliyah opened the door with tears dripping off of her chin and she was reeking of Vodka. As soon as she saw me she dropped the bottle and collapsed into my arms, sobbing loudly. "He killed my mother, Rich. I told you he wasn't to be played with. He killed my mother, and now he looking for me all over the city. What am I going to do?" She groaned.

I picked her up and carried her to the bed while she broke down, shaking as if she was losing her mind. "It's gon' be okay, Aaliyah. I got you. We gon' figure out what's going on," I promised. The heavy scent of liquor and her cycle roamed up my nose. I figured that it must've been a while since she'd had a bath, so I laid her back. "Chill for one second, okay?"

She broke down a little harder and covered her face with her hands as she laid on her back.

I got up, jogged into the bathroom and ran some warm bath water before coming back into the room and slowly stripping her out of her clothes, one piece at a time while she cried and cried.

"I loved her so much, Rich. She was all that I had left. Now what am I going to do? It's all my fault," she whimpered, and continued to allow for me to strip her. That part I couldn't believe.

"I know, Aaliyah. We gon' figure it out. I'mma handle that nigga for you. But for right now, you gotta take a bath, ma. You don't smell so good."

After she was naked, I picked her up and she wrapped her right arm around my neck. I carried her to the bathroom where she sat on the toilet and pullet out her tampon, placing it into the plastic bag that I had waiting for her. Then, she sat on the toilet and peed before I picked her back up and slowly lowered her into the bath water.

Taking a towel and lathering it with soap, I took her arm and began the process of washing her entire body from head to toe while she cried and told me how she was feeling.

"I feel sick, Rich. I hate Ken so much. I've always hated him. My mother didn't have anything to do with what went on between me and Meeka. He's nothing but a bully, and one day he's going to reap what he's sewn."

I knew I didn't have the right words to say to her. I could only imagine what she was going through. Her mother had just been murdered by a man that she felt had her trapped. I don't think there was anything that I could say to make her feel better, so I continued to wash her body in silence while tears rolled down her cheeks.

After I made her stand up, so the shower water could wash off all of the dirt and grime, I watched her put her tampon back in. Then, I picked her up and carried her back to the bed, softly laying her on it.

She took the clean sheets that I'd bought her from Walmart and pulled them over her body. "Rich, I know you have to leave and everything, but I really don't want to be alone for a while. I'm so afraid. Can you please hold me until I fall asleep? I need to be in your loving arms, if that's okay." She looked me in the eyes.

I nodded, taking a second to kick off my black and gray Jordan's before climbing on to the bed, laying on my side and pulling her close to me, placing my chin on the top of her head. I could
smell the coconut scented shampoo and conditioner that I'd used to scrub her scalp with.

She waited for me to take hold of her before she lifted the sheets and pulled them upward, exposing her naked body from behind. "Get under here with me, Rich. Don't be afraid."

I laughed and slid under the covers with her, feeling her naked body mold to my chest and stomach. I placed my chin back on the top of her head and closed my eyes, making sure that I held her nice and firmly. She felt good in my arms, I can't even lie.

"I'll do anything, Rich, to have you get rid of Ken for me. I know that you're a hustler, and I can put you up on a lick that will get you all the way right. Trust me when I tell you this," she said, scooting backward until her booty was in my lap.

It felt soft and warm. I tried my best to think unsex like thoughts, but I was finding it so hard because Aaliyah was so cold and was a long-time crush. She was one of those females that you always imagined yourself laying in the bed with, but in the back of your mind you never thought it would come true. I knew I had to restrain myself because, first off, she was on her cycle, and secondly, her mother had just been murdered. Only a scumbag would've tried to go in on her at a time like that. I just needed to be there for emotional support, but the talk of a lick did have my ears open wide.

"What you talking about, lil' mama?" I asked, inhaling her womanly scent a lil' bit.

She snuggled back into me and sighed. "I've never had a man just hold me before. Especially not while I was on my period. It feels nice." She was quiet for a second. She moved backward into me, took my hand and placed it on her hip. "I got this trick, a white man, that's real heavy into narcotics. Every time he fucks me, he takes me out to his mansion in West Allis. You know, on the south side of town. It's like Scarface lives there or something. There is coke and heroin all over the place. I've seen bricks of it. That and weed, but I'm pretty sure that doesn't interest you."

I moved my head around until my cheek was laying on top of hers. "Don't try and overthink things. Just give me the information that you have and allow for me to make my own decisions, okay?"

She smiled and rubbed her cheek against mine a lil' bit. "This is so nice. You smell good, too. I love it." She exhaled loudly. "Okay, well he usually meets up with me two times out of the month, and he's the only trick that I have that Ken doesn't know about. I've kept him a secret for my own selfish reasons. We'll get into those at another time. However, I am willing to set him up for you, so you can get all of his goods. If you do things the right way you can walk away with so much dope that you'll never have to work the block again. You'll be a king. All I ask is that you, in turn, kill Ken for me. That way I'll be free, and he'll be forced to pay for what he's done to my mother. She didn't deserve to die, and I don't deserve to be in fear for my life. What do you say?"

I started to rub the side of her hip for a minute, collecting my thoughts. What she was proposing sounded real good to my ears, but almost too good to be true. I started to wonder if she was selling me a dream just, so I could knock Ken off for her, and if she was, it was something that she didn't have to do because I was already considering murking him anyway. One thing I disliked was a liar. I tried my best to keep shit one hunnit at all times. Lying to me was a good way for me to quit messing with you on all levels. I didn't care who you were.

"Aaliyah, you know we just getting to know each other and everything, and I don't want to come at you bogus or make you feel like I don't trust you or nothing like that, but I just gotta protect myself, nah'mean?"

She sat up and turned around to face me. "Rich, stop all that beating around the bush shit and say what's on your mind. I feel like you know enough about me that you can keep shit real and let me know what you're thinking at all times. So, spit it out."

I sat up and exhaled loudly, running my hands over my face. "A'ight, look. For Ken, if you blowing smoke to get me to knock that nigga off, you ain't got to. Just on the strength of how me and him had an ugly run in, I'm gon' take care of him, so you're good."

She frowned. "Wait. What do you mean blowing smoke? What? You think I'm lying to you about the lick or something?"

I shrugged and looked into her eyes without saying a word.

She sucked her teeth and got out of the bed, wrapping a sheet around her naked frame before walking back and forth, lookin' at the floor. "Damn, so I guess since I sold a lil' pussy that gives you the right to think I'm dishonest, and that I'll play you like some two-dollar whore, huh?" She blew air through her teeth and shook her head. "Wow."

I got out of the bed and dusted myself off, picking up one of my shoes and putting it on my foot. I ain't feel like arguing with no female. That just wasn't my thing. I tried my best to be as respectful as I could when it came to them because within every female I saw a version of my mother or little sisters.

"Look, I ain't mean no disrespect by it. Like I said, I was just protecting myself because I represent a picture that's bigger than my own. I got a lot of vulnerable loved ones depending on me to make it happen, which is why I have to dissect everything that this game brings. It's unfortunate, but it's my life."

Aaliyah lowered her head and bit into her bottom lip. "I guess I can respect that." She walked across the room until she was standing in front of me with her head leaned to the side, looking into my eyes with her pretty face. She was without make up. She looked pure and a bit younger, even though there were bags under her eyes.

I reached out with my thumb and ran it across them. I don't know why I wanted to feel her there, but I did. I grabbed her cheeks and brought her forehead to my lips, kissing her right in the middle of it.

"Mmm-a." She closed her eyes and stood on her tippy toes, so she could feel it better. "I've never met a dude as affectionate as you are. It's so rare, and it makes me feel so good. I'm getting weaker over you and I know it ain't cool because don't you have a girl?" She looked up at me, waiting for my response.

I rubbed the side of her soft cheek with the back of the fingers on my right hand. "Yeah, it's something like that. I got somebody in my life that I care about, but we ain't got no labels or nothin', though she is special to me."

She lowered her head in defeat. "That is what I was afraid of. I feel like you're going to make me fall in love with you, and then you're going to kick me to the curb for a female that doesn't have as much of a history as I do. And you wanna know what? If you did something like that I couldn't even blame you. Who'd want to be with a girl that once sold pussy? Most dudes are looking for young females just, so they can pop their cherries. Life sucks." She exhaled and walked away from me. "I want to show you something to prove what I'm saying to you is the truth." She grabbed her phone and started to type on it before turning it sideways and handing it over to me. "When I was working for Ken, he had this thing where he always had to go through our phones and know our codes for everything, but he wasn't the brightest bulb, so it was easy to keep things from him. Check out those pictures."

I grabbed the iPhone and looked at the first picture. It was of a table full of cocaine or what appeared to be cocaine, because next to the powdery substance was four wrapped packages with an Uncle Sam stamp on them. I swiped, and the next picture was of what appeared to be ten packages stacked up against a wall. I kept on swiping until different colored packages appeared on the screen.

"I haven't lied to you since we've officially met, Rich, and I don't feel the need to. Now I know for a fact that this white man is obsessed with me, and I can set him up so that you walk away with all of his dope. All you have to do is murder Ken's punk ass." She grabbed the phone back from me. "I know you can make some major money off that shit. My cousin's baby father down in Chicago will fuck with you real tough too. Once upon a time I thought about putting him up on the move, but I didn't see any benefit in it for me. He runs shit down in the Windy City though. He has an army of niggas that follow behind him." She sat on the bed and looked over at me. "So, what do you think?"

I was already imagining how me, and Paper could pull of that lick. It looked like at least twenty plus bricks in there, and if that was the case then we would be set for a minute. I felt like we could go hard for the summer and by the time the winter came I'd have enough to put some serious funds into my sisters' savings accounts. That way, when it was time for them to go off to college, they would be set.

I walked over to Aaliyah and sat on the bed beside her. "How you get them pictures? Is dude really a lame like that?" I just wanted to know the type of man I was dealing with.

She smiled. "He trusts me, Rich. Pussy will do some things to a man. if you know what you're doing with it." She giggled and looked away all shy like.

"Alright, I'll tell you what. We gon' hit this lick with this white dude or whatever, and directly after that, I'm gon' hunt that nigga Ken down and clap his ass. One hand will wash the other, and you'll be free from that punk."

"What about afterwards? Are we going to still be cool or is this more of a business arrangement, where you look out for me and I look out for you? Do you feel any sparks coming from between us?" she asked, taking her hand and placing it on the back of my neck to rub it slowly yet delicately.

I laughed at that. "I'm feeling you, Aaliyah. I like yo' swag and I know you've been through a lot. I'm gon' try my best to be there for you, even after all of this is concluded. You got my word on that." I got out of the bed and put my other shoe on. I wanted to get over to Paper's trap, so I could run this move by him in person.

"Tell me a secret, Rich."

I stopped in the middle of tying my laces and looked over to her. "What you just say to me?"

She sat up more straight in the bed, peering into my eyes from a distance. "You're a very peculiar individual. You're not like most men. I can't seem to pick you apart mentally, so I want you to let me in there just a little bit. So, come on now. You know a whole lot about me and I don't know anything about you at all. So, tell me something. One of your deepest secrets that makes you the way you are. You know, before we enter into this new phase of things. Please." She adjusted herself nervously.

I finished putting my Jordan's back on, stood up and rolled my head around on my neck before placing my pistol into the small of my back. Then, I walked over to her and sat beside her once again. I didn't even know what I was telling her until I finished. I took a deep breath. "You remember that I told you that my mother passed away from an overdose of heroin, right?"

She nodded and cleared her throat. "Yeah, I do."

I rolled my head around on my neck again as I felt my eyes get watery. My throat got tight and I felt like I had a lump inside of it. "Well, I'm the reason that she overdosed," I said barely above a whisper.

She gasped, swallowed and reached out and took my hand. A lone tear had fallen down my cheek. I quickly wiped it away. I was the typa nigga that dried tears, not shed them. "It's okay, Rich. Just tell me what you mean. I'm here for you." She wrapped her arm around my shoulder and pulled me to her breast.

I allowed for my cheek to rest on its softness. There was nothing like the comfort of a woman. The tears cascaded down my face and onto her sheet.

I swallowed the lump. "I gave her that final dose that killed her. Had I not, she would've still been alive and walking to this day."

At saying the last part, I fell to my knees, imagining my mother's face as she began to overdose off of the doses of heroin that I'd given her nearly a year ago. I saw the way the foam rose in her mouth until it pooled out of her and down her chin. I felt my stomach turn upside down as I recalled that tragic night.

Aaliyah got out of the bed and kneeled beside me, rubbing my back. She leaned over and kissed me on the cheek. "It's okay, Rich. I know you didn't mean to do it. You don't need to beat yourself up over this." She turned my head so that I was looking directly at her. Then she reached and rubbed my tears away, looking into my eyes.

I closed them and lowered my head, taking a deep breath so I could get ahold of myself. I wasn't the type to shed tears, especially not in front of other people. I was the type that usually went and wrote my thoughts and feelings down. It was the way I expressed them. By this point, I had already written so many short stories about the things that had taken place in my life that I had a laptop full of them.

I exhaled loudly and shook my head. "I miss my mother so much, Aaliyah. I ain't even get the chance to say goodbye to her. I was too busy expecting for her to pull through. I never took the time out to face the reality of me and her situation."

Aaliyah continued to rub my cheeks with her thumbs, and that felt weird because I was used to being the one to console other people by wiping their tears away using that method.

I felt a little emasculated because I'd heard somewhere that men weren't supposed to cry. I think it was one of the reasons prior to this point that I'd never shed a tear over my mother, even though every single day since it happened I felt the need to.

"Rich, you didn't know that those doses were going to be her last, and what you have to understand is that if she had not gotten them from you she would have gotten them from somebody else. I mean, I know that's not that reassuring, but it's the one hundred percent truth." She looked into my eyes for a long time, then leaned in and kissed me on the cheek, rubbing her face against my own in an affectionate manner.

I fully faced her and wrapped my arms around her small frame, taking the back of her head and pushing it forward so that she was laying on my chest. "Yo, I appreciate you saying that and for you allowing me to open up to you. I see that it ain't easy, and I commend you for giving me so much of yourself, seriously." I hugged her and kissed her cheek, stroking her hair.

"Rich, I know it's early, but I'm telling you that in the end it's going to be me and you. There is this energy between us that's undeniable. I'm not trying to force anything, but just beware." She raised her head, and for the first time, she kissed me on the lips, taking her hand and holding the side of my face, sucking on first my bottom one and then the top.

It took me a few seconds to get into the act because her kiss had caught me off guard. When her lips first met mine,

I honestly started to think about the street life that she was in. You know, the countless men that she'd probably been in contact with. Then, I thought about Andrea and how she made me feel. So, I felt a lil' guilty because Andrea had been so one hunnit to me. But then it was like I felt something from her kiss— a lil' spark or something like that, and it made me want to return her affections, so I did.

As she sucked my top lip, I sucked her bottom one, then her tongue swiped at mine before we started to simply go at it. We were breathing hard into each other's mouths all lusty and shit. I didn't even notice that she'd dropped her sheet until I felt her naked breasts pressing into my chest, both nipples spiked out. I grabbed them into my hands and squeezed them, loving the feel of their weight as she sucked all over my neck.

Then out of the blue, I pulled back and held her at arm's length, shaking my head. "We can't get down like this, Aaliyah. We gotta keep the emotions out of it until we handle our business on both ends. It'll make things so much simpler," I said, even though my dick was rock hard.

I couldn't allow for us to mix business with pleasure because at the end of the day, the business aspect was more important. I had my whole household on my back, and at this point Aaliyah's life was on the line, and so was her freedom.

She sucked on her bottom lip and wiped away my saliva from the top of her upper one. She pulled the sheet around her body and looked me over with lusty eyes. She nodded. "Maybe you're right." She stood up and turned her back to me, leaned over and picked up her panties, sliding them up her legs. "I'm gon' get things in order on my end, and I'll be at you. Just be ready when I call, and we'll take it from there. Okay?" She turned around to face me, and I tried my hardest to not look over them pretty titties with the big, chocolate areolas.

"I will be. You got my word on that." I stepped forward and pulled her into my embrace. "And don't think I ain't hear everything that you said because I did. I feel the same things that you feel and trust me it was hard for me to stop back there, but we have to. At least for right now. A'ight?" I hugged her tighter.

She nodded. "In the end, its gon' be me and you. Just watch."

HOOD RICH

Chapter 12

I was sitting at the table in Paper's trap, a day after me and Aaliyah had come to our understanding, when there was a loud banging on the backdoor.

Paper and I had been chopping down and bagging up half a kilo of Andrea's mixture when he jumped up and took his latex gloves off of his hands and placed them on the table beside his pile of dope. "Man, these fiends act like they can't wait the lil' three hours until we open shop back up. This shit crazy." He laughed, and I knew he meant crazy in a good way because the night before I'd dropped him off nine ounces, and in less than two hours they were all gone.

We were chopping down the half a kilo getting ourselves prepared for Shirley's party that was set to take place at eleven that night, and we were halfway done.

Paper cocked his Glock and put it on his hip. "I'll be back, bruh. Let me go serve these fiends." He snatched up about ten rocks and headed to the backdoor of the trap before opening it and going down the stairs.

I continued to bag up our work. I wanted to be finished so I could get back home and take a nice long shower. It had been about two days and I was starting to feel icky.

Shirley came into the living room where we were, yawning with her hands stretched over her head. She walked up to me and wrapped her arms around my neck, hugging me. "Afternoon, nephew. How you feeling, baby?"

I smiled. "I'm good, TT. How about yourself?" I knew that she was trying to get me all mushy and shit, so she could wiggle in and get a bag for free, so I just cut to the chase and handed her one. "Here."

She took it out of my hand and took a step back, looking down at it with a big smile on her face. "Shit, I'm doing good now. Thank you, baby." She hugged me again and disappeared into her room that Paper allowed for her to stay in from time to time.

I still couldn't believe that he was fucking her, but to each its own, I guessed.

I placed about four hundred dime bags in a big Ziploc when I looked up and saw Jamie walking into the living room with Paper behind him. On Paper's face was a look of irritation.

Jamie curled his upper lip and looked over the table before pulling a chair from under it, mugging me with hatred. "What's good, Rich? I see you doing your thing all of the sudden. When did all of this come about?" He picked up about ten rocks and allowed them to fall to the table again.

I felt my head begin to heat up. I shot my hand forward and scooted the dope away from him. "This shit don't concern you, old man. Stay in yo' lane and I'll stay in mine." I mugged the shit out of him and lowered my eyes. I never really liked Jamie because he had this habit of looking at people like they weren't shit, and back in the days when I really wasn't doing so well, I felt like he was looking down on me. I didn't like nobody looking down on me because in my heart I've always been a proud person.

Jamie grunted and slammed his hand on the table loudly. "This shit got everything to do with me, especially if it's my son's blood that allowed for this to take place." He sucked his teeth and looked me in the eye, challengingly.

Paper walked around the table to my right shoulder and mugged him. "Nigga, I told you we ain't got shit to do with yo' son getting kilt, now you can quit coming at my nigga like it's sweet or something, or a muhfucka gon' have to show you what's really good. That's on my mama." Paper said. I could see his eyes getting red which meant that his temper was rising like my own.

I shook my head. "N'all, don't tell this nigga shit. Let him keep on trying me and he'll find out what's good soon enough."

Jamie looked from me to Paper then back to me. "Man, you lil' bitch ass niggas. Ain't y'all the same muhfuckas that Fax laid down just last summer? Now y'all all hard and shit, huh?" He laughed with a frown on his face, looking deep into my eyes, then slowly trailed them to Paper. "Lil' nigga, if I didn't care about your mother in the way that I do, I'da knocked you off a long time ago. I never liked you and I still don't. I know you living foul lil' boy, and when I find out that you're the one that set my son up, I'm gon' slay yo' punk ass and keep on fuckin' your mother, how you love that?" He laughed out loud with his upper lip curled.

I looked over at Paper with my eyes bugged out of my head. In my opinion, that was the ultimate disrespect. Not only was he bragging about fucking his mother, but he was basically telling him that somewhere down the line that he was going to kill him.

Paper got ready to say something, and I don't know what he was finna say, but before he could get his words out I swung and punched Jamie so hard that he flew backward out of the chair and hit his head on the wooden floor.

I jumped out of my chair, straddling him, punching him again and again in the nose and mouth. "You. Bitch. Ass.

Nigga. You. Gon'. Respect. My. Nigga. And. His. Moms."
I said, fucking him up, watching his blood pop into the air.

His head bounced off of the floorboards and he failed
to protect himself. I think after the first couple blows that
he was already knocked out and sleeping, but you couldn't
tell my brain that. I hated this bitch ass nigga. I didn't give
a fuck if Paper had murked his son or not, Paper was like
my brother. I wasn't about to let nobody talk that bullshit
to him or disrespect his mother's honor. It just wasn't
happening.

Shirley ran out of the room and saw what I was doing
and smiled wickedly. "Kill him, nephew. Kill his bitch ass.
I hate that muthafucka!" She hollered.

My knuckles slammed into his face again and again. I
was out of breath and my vision was hazy by the time it
became clear again, Paper was pulling me off of him.

"Yo, chill, Rich. That nigga is out. Look at him!" he
hollered, pointing down at Jamie.

Jamie laid flat on his back with his eyes wide open and
blood coming out of his nose and mouth. His chest heaved,
signifying that he was alive, and I wouldn't have been mad
if he hadn't been.

I pushed Paper up off me. "Why you let his bitch ass in
here anyway, knowing that we had all this dope on the
table?" I asked, feeling like going over and stomping
Jamie. I watched him cough up a bloody loogey, trying to
spit it out but it slid down his chin and stayed there.

Paper ran his hand over his deep waves and shook his
head. "I wasn't thinking, bruh. Word is bond, I wasn't." He
looked down at Jamie as the man tried to sit up.

He shook and turned to his side before coming to his
feet. I got ready to finish him off. I didn't like seeing him
be able to get up.

136

Shirley ran into his face and bumped her chest against his. "That's what the fuck you get, Jamie. You ain't nothing but a big ass bully anyway. I'll never forget what you did to me back in the day." She spits in his face before smacking him with all of her might.

He stumbled into the wall, went under his shirt and came up with a nine-millimeter, cocking it back and aiming the gun at her with a mug on his face. Blood ran from his nose in rivers.

I upped my .38 Special and aimed it at him. Then, I looked to my right and saw that Paper had two Glocks aimed at him as well. "Yo, you shoot her, I'm stanking you, nigga." I said, walking over to them. As soon as I was close enough I pulled Shirley behind me. She'd had her hands in the air looking terrified. "Take yo' ass in that room, Aunty, now!" I ordered.

She nodded and slowly backed her way into the bedroom she often slept in and closed the door. "Kill that nigga, Rich. He needs to be in the ground. I swear to God he do."

Jamie faced me and aimed his gun at my head. I cocked the hammer on my pistol and got ready to dance with his bitch ass. I was tired of playing around with him. He spat a bloody loogey on the floor. "Look, man, you ain't have to do this to me, Rich. I ain't never put my hands on you."

I frowned. "Fuck all this talking. What you gon' do with that gun raised like that? You gon' shoot, or you gon' keep saying shit to me that don't mean nothing?"

Paper stepped alongside of me with his guns raised. "Get the fuck out the trap, Jamie. This yo' last chance. We ain't have shit to do with yo' son getting killed, and muhfuckas don't want shit to do with you. Now, step. Now!" He ordered, cocking his hammers.

Jamie swallowed and slowly walked backward. "A'ight, it's good. I'm just gon' go on about my business. Act like this day never happened. Y'all don't say shit to me from here on out, and I won't say shit to y'all." He continued to walk backward toward the door until he was going down the steps and out of the house after Paper opened the door for him, so he could retreat.

Looking back at this day now, I see that it was one of the worst mistakes I had ever made because I underestimated this man. I allowed for my anger to cloud my judgement. When all of this happened, me and Paper should have killed him right then, because if we had then Jamie wouldn't have had the opportunity to cause us so much chaos, heartache and pain.

Shirley came out of the room as soon as she heard the backdoor slam shut. "Y'all should've kilt that rapist son of a bitch. I'm telling you this shit ain't over. Y'all should've never let him walk away like that. He'll be back. Trust me when I tell you this. That nigga will be back for blood, and he ain't gon' stop coming until somebody kill his ass." She shook her head and took a rock off of the table without asking for it.

As much as I wanted to feed into what Shirley was screaming, I ignored it to a fault, and twenty minutes later I pulled away from Paper's trap, so I could go to Andrea's house and take a shower. My mind was all over the place as I rolled to the crib. I was thinking about the words that had come out of Shirley's mouth, and I knew that I had made a mistake by allowing for Jamie to walk out of there. Especially after finding out that back in the day he'd raped Shirley on multiple occasions. I felt sorry for her and I hated him even more because of it. Even though she really wasn't any kin to me, I still didn't like imagining her going

138

through something so traumatic. Nobody deserved that. Then on top that off, Jamie didn't seem like the type that would take a loss without crying foul or getting back at the person as hard as he could. Me and Paper had to murk this nigga. There was no way around it. Our lives depended on it.

Even though I had that whole situation on my brain, I couldn't stop thinking about Aaliyah. I missed her, I worried about her, and I felt like I just needed to be around her a little more. She made me feel so normal because of all of the things that she and I had been through separately. I felt like I had somebody in my life that finally understood my pains and wouldn't judge me for my poor decisions. I felt a need for her, and I couldn't deny the attraction because it was so strong, and it surpassed the physical aspect of want.

I shook my head and rolled my window down, so I could get some good old fresh air. It was one of those days outside where it was real sunny, but it wasn't too hot or unbearable. I let the wind blow into my face as I tried to get control of my thoughts. By the time I pulled on to Andrea's block, I was as cool as a fan and had concluded that Jamie had to go that night after Shirley's party, and that I would explore something deeper with Aaliyah, even though I didn't know quite what it was.

So, I was calm and collected with a clear head until I got about four houses away from Andrea's and spotted Ken's truck parked in front of our house. My first thought was that he was there looking for Aaliyah, and I knew it was about to be some bullshit because I couldn't control my temper around this bitch nigga. I curled my lip as I pulled up behind his truck and threw my car into park. I looked all around the block and saw that there were plenty people out on their porches, on the sidewalks jumping rope, sipping cups of lemonade and all sorts of other things. The last thing I needed to make was a scene, so I took a bunch of deep breaths and calmed down as best I could before opening my car door and stepping out of it.

At the same time, Ken's passenger's door opened, and imagine how I felt when Keyonna stepped out of it before she closed the door and he pulled off with his system banging loudly. She looked over to me and her entire face flushed red before she smiled weakly and made her way up the stairs to Andrea's house, wearing a Prada skirt so short that it rose nearly to her hips by the time she was on the top stair.

I slammed my car door and shot up the stairs so fast that I almost fell on a few of them. Before she opened the door, I grabbed a hand full of her hair and forced her ass into the house. It was the first time I had ever did anything like that, but in my opinion, it was warranted.

She snapped her head backward and tried to remove my fingers from out of her scalp. "Let me go, Rich, what's your problem?"

I tightened my grip and got to walking through the house with her, leading her to her bedroom. We passed Kesha who was sitting at the table doing her homework, and Andrea, who was in the kitchen cooking dinner. They looked at me with eyes wide open but didn't say a word.

Soon as we got to Keyonna's bedroom, I threw her inside and closed the door behind me. She wound up falling on the bed, on to her stomach, letting out a yelp. I took my pistol off of me and put it into her top drawer, then slid my Gucci belt from around my waist. "Keyonna, I'mma ask you one time and one time only, and you better tell me the truth. What were you doing in that truck with Ken?"

She turned over to face me. I noticed that her skirt was pulled all the way up to her waist, exposing her lace, red boy short panties. That pissed me off even more so. She neglected to pull it back down as she explained herself. "That wasn't Ken, Rich, that was his son Kendell, and I've been going out with him for three months now. Why is it all of the sudden a problem?" she asked, looking terrified.

I pointed. "Pull yo' skirt down, Keyonna, and tell me that you ain't been that careless the whole time you been wearing it." I said, feeling myself becoming heated.

She laid on her back and wiggled her body as she pulled the skirt down her thighs. "No, I haven't. I was so scared right now that I didn't even notice that."

I exhaled, ran my hand over my waves and shook my head. "I don't want you fucking with Kendall no more. Him or Ken. Both of them niggas is foul and I ain't about to have them around you. That's that." I pursed my lips and flared my nostrils, heated from imagining anybody from Ken's bloodline all over my sister. I knew I was gon' kill this nigga now. I had to take my anger out on his ass.

Keyonna blew air through her nose and crossed her arms in front of her chest, looking away from me. "You don't even know Kendell like that. He's nothing like his father. He goes to church and everything."

"Look, Keyonna, I'm not about to have this conversation with you. Now, it's over between you and dude. I don't wanna catch you with him no more. If I do, I'm gon' whoop yo' lil' ass like I'm supposed to; you hear me?" I asked, walking closer to the bed with my belt in my hand in a threatening manner.

I didn't know if I would actually whoop my sister, but at that time I was mad enough to do so because I felt like she was in danger and was too naive to actually see that. I knew that more often than not, pimps used younger boys and girls to recruit their prey, and I felt like Ken was using his son to do just that, and I refused to let my sister fall victim to that process. I loved her way too much and I wasn't going for it.

She was quiet and pouting at the same time. "I love him, Rich. I love him so much, and it's not fair for you to keep him away from me. He's been nothing but good to me." She turned on to her stomach and cried into her pillow loudly.

Andrea knocked on the door and opened it without getting permission to do so. "What's going on in here?" She asked looking from me to her. She stepped further into the room and made her way toward the bed. She sat on it and rubbed Keyonna's back.

I held up my hand. "I'm handling it, so you good. She heard what I said and I'm not playing." I felt my heart pounding in my chest. I had to get out of that room or I was going to whoop my sister's ass.

She turned over to face Andrea with tears in her eyes. "He wants me to stay away from Kendell because of what his father does, and it isn't fair. I'm a grown woman and my brother treats me like a child." She stuck her head back under the pillow and continued to cry while Andrea shook her head and rubbed her back.

"Rich, maybe you two should get an understanding. I mean, she is a grown woman now, and we have to trust her more. What do you say?"

Keyonna turned over with tears running down her cheeks to see what I was about to say, and I know I crushed her soul when I waved Andrea off and frowned. "What I said is final. If I catch her with that nigga again, I'm tearing her ass up. That dude ain't right, whether she can see it or not."

"Ahhh! I hate it here!" were the last words that were hollered pertaining to that subject.

HOOD RICH

Chapter 13

Paper came into the room and handed me a bundle of cash with a big smile on his face. "This seven bands, my nigga. Seven gees and the party ain't even got started yet." He hollered, "Let's get this money!" He picked up a Ziploc bag and left out of his bedroom, or the room that he often slept in whenever he stayed a night in the trap.

I took the seven bands and placed them within the safe that I'd picked up a week ago before closing it and snatching up my own Ziploc bag full of rocks. After they were tucked safely in my underwear, I left the room and placed the lock on the door and hit up the party just as twenty dope addicts were coming in through the backdoor. All of them with large bills in their hands.

Shirley ushered them into the living room where we'd placed a bunch of couch pillows on the floor for them to sit for their comfort while they smoked until their money ran out. "Y'all, follow me and prepare to have a good old time. This is my day and I don't want no bullshit. It's all about having fun and celebrating me. Yesss!" she said, dancing to the Isley Brothers song that was booming out of the speakers.

I watched the new group of dope heads take their place on the floor before Paper came up to serve them. They handed him their money and he handed them an ashtray and a package of magnum condoms.

I laughed at that and started to make my rounds, serving as many fiends as I could, racking up thousands of dollars in just a few hours. I had a doctor's mask covering my nose and mouth because the dope smoke was so thick in the air that it made it hard for me to breathe. Plus, I wasn't trying to catch no contact from that shit.

About three hours after the party had been cracking and everybody seemed to be smoked out, Shirley walked up to me with a beer in her hand, dancing to the Isley Brothers' song *Groove With You*, stepping from side to side all cool like. She reached out and tried to take my hand, but I wasn't with it. I had to keep my eyes on everything because Paper was acting like he had a contact or something.

"You ain't gon' dance with yo' Aunty on her birthday, baby?" She asked turning in a circle and sliding to the side.

A male dope addict walked up to me and handed me five one hundred-dollar bills. "Do me right, baby boy." He scratched his neck. "I been waiting all month for this day." He smacked his lips together, took Shirley's hand and started to dance with her.

I reached into the bag and counted him off fifty dime bags and gave them to him while he held his hands together to receive them.

Shirley wrapped her arm around his neck and kissed his cheek. "Now you know you gotta make sure the birthday girl is straight. That's the rule of my party, and that's how it goes. Pay up, muthafucka." She smiled, turned around and rubbed her ass all into his crotch.

He held his dope over her head, turned his back on her and walked back into the living room while nodding. "Unless you giving me some of that wet shit, ain't nothing happening. You owe me some pussy, you know it," were the last words I heard before they disappeared into the living room.

I walked all around the trap catching money and watching the hypes fuck and smoke until they were coughing up their lungs. They laughed and joked all loudly, while some played dominos and Spades. I went out and bought four big ass bags of KFC chicken to make sure that they ate, or at least it was available for them to eat, along with five cases of Wild Wood sodas.

The party lasted until eight in the morning the next day, and after it was all said and done, we made a $110,000. That was after I deducted what it cost for us to supply them with food, drinks and condoms. I walked away with fifty-five gees, all of which I put into my safe that I kept in Andrea's basement.

***

Later that night, as it was raining harder than I ever remembered, I jumped into Paper's whip with murder on my mind. He pulled away from the curb and handed me a black Glock that held seventeen bullets, and I intended on using as many of them as it would take to wipe Jamie off of the earth.

He pushed in his car's lighter. "My mother staying over my aunt's house tonight because my aunty Kathy ain't been feeling well. I know we shouldn't body this nigga at my mother's crib, but fuck that. It's now or never and everything you said make sense. We'd be a damn fool to let this nigga keep on living knowing that we killed his son, and you just whooped his ass, to add insult to his injuries."

I cocked the Glock and placed it on my hip. "Exactly. We should've murked that nigga the same night we slayed his kid. We gotta remember that we can't be leaving no lose ends. That's tacky and that'll get us fucked over, quick." I shook my head. "We starting to get money now. The last thing we need is this muhfucka being a problem." I rolled up my window all the way because it had been open a crack and some of the rain was leaking onto my face. I wiped it away and looked over at Paper as he took the car's lighter and lit his cigarette. I didn't want to smell that shit. I hated the smell of cigarettes because it always made my head hurt.

He took two pills and popped them, then chased them with the apple juice from his cup holder. "I got us some lil' young niggas to work the trap, too. These lil' niggas thorough. I just copped two more spots that we can hustle out of, and I want to open them up right away. One on Twenty-Eighth and Chambers, and the other one on Twenty-Ninth and Concordia. The fiends in both of those hoods pay up, so we need to expand out in those directions, nah'mean?"

I nodded and looked out of my window. I still had murder on my mind and I was trying to get myself prepared to take a life. For me that shit wasn't as easy as they made it seem in the movies. It was a mental battle that took some time to overcome. "Where you meet these lil' dudes at?"

He shook his head and pulled off of the square. "They from around the hood. The lil' homeys go to Auer Avenue school. I think they like eleven or twelve. Either way, they know how to get money and I'm gon' use they lil' ass to help us get rich. They juveniles which mean that they can't do no jail time. It'll mostly be slaps on the wrist, and all we gotta do is buy they ass a video game and they'll stay in the trap all day hustling for us. Shit, all we'd have to do is collect, and ain't that what it's all about?" He pulled off of the square again and blew the smoke out.

I felt like I was ready to throw up all over the dashboard. That smell of his square had me nauseous. "Bruh, put that stankin' ass cigarette out. That shit killing my head." I felt dizzy and all type of shit.

Paper rolled down his window and threw the square out of it. Rain splashed into the car until he rolled it back up. "You so damn dramatic, that shit is almost comical."

We rolled in silence for the next twenty minutes. I assumed that we had so much on our minds that it was a struggle to keep focused. I felt the butterflies in my stomach, on top of it was the feeling as if I had to take a dump. My stomach was doing somersaults. I tried my best to calm down by taking nonchalant deep breaths and blowing them out slowly. I just wanted to get this night over and one with. I had such a bad feeling in my gut.

We wound up parking a block away from Paper's mother's house. Paper turned off the ignition, exhaled loudly, took his guns and cocked them before putting them back on to his waistband and sitting back in his seat. "You ready to handle this business, nigga?" He asked, looking over at me.

The steady sound of rain pouring down onto the hood of the car and windshield was causing me to get lost in its rhythm for a while before I regained my focus. "Yeah, let's do this, bruh, and get it over with so we can get back to chasing this cash. I wanna take my sisters on a vacation this summer. You know, spoil them a lil' bit. They deserve it, nah'mean?"

Keyonna's face popped into my mind. The last time I'd seen her, she was giving me a look that said she hated my guts and that she'd never forgive me. I knew that she thought that I was just trying to control her and not looking out for her best interest, and I just prayed that in time she would understand. Until then, I would continue to love her and protect her with everything that I was.

Paper nodded. "Yeah, that sound like a plan. Maybe we'll hit up Hawaii or something; leave the hood for a while."

I liked the sound of that. Five minutes later, after we gathered ourselves, we were running down the alley while the rain attacked us violently and thunder roared in the sky, followed by flashes of lightning. By the time we made it to the side of Paper's mother's house, I was drenched and so was he, but never the less we were focused.

Paper had purposely left his bedroom window open for us to climb into, and it's just what we did, one by one— first him and then me. We fell to his carpet and rolled to stand. I took my pistol off of my hip and looked him over, waiting for him to take charge because it was his house. That was until we heard a loud smack, followed by a scream and the sound of dishes breaking. My ears perked up on high alert.

"Please! Don't do this, Jamie! I'm sorry!" Another slap. This time, louder than the one before it.

Paper swung open the door to his bedroom and ran out of it before I could hold him back, not that I was looking too anyway. The next thing I knew, he was running into the kitchen with me behind him. As soon as he got there, he took the side of his gun and smacked the shit out of Jamie with it, causing him to let his mother go.

Jamie had had her pinned up against the wall by her throat, choking her with both hands. The attack from Paper made him drop her and he flew into the stove awkwardly. Within seconds Paper was on top of him with his gun turned upside down, beating him in the head with the handle again and again.

Paper's mother, whose name was Nelly, fell to the floor then jumped up and screamed as she watched her son beat her husband senseless. "Demetrius! Demetrius! Stop it, you're killing him, baby. He ain't gon' hit me no more, I swear!" She hollered as she reached down and tried to pull Paper off of him.

Paper stood for a second just to shake her off, then he sat back down and continued to beat Jamie over the head with the gun while he kicked out at the air. "I told you. I told you. Never. Put. Yo'. Hands. On. My. Mother!"

Over and over, I watched Jamie's head open up. The wounds that I'd given him only a short while ago had never gotten the chance to properly heal. With a strike of Paper's gun's butt, they were forced open, leaking his blood all over the linoleum floor.

"Aye! Get the fuck off of him!" I heard from over my shoulder. It was the first time that I'd been made aware that his mother and Jamie had not been the only ones in the house. I turned around to see Fax sitting at their dining room table along with two other men.

Me and Fax made eye contact before he grabbed the piles of money that were on top of the table and stuffed them into his duffle bag. I also noted that on top of the table was three kilos of dope. Fax took them one at a time, stuffing them into his bag along with the money.

The two men pulled out pistols and aimed them directly into the kitchen. I fell to my ass, aimed my gun at them and started shooting just as the first one let off two shots. *Boom. Boom.* The first bullet flew past my shoulder and slammed into the back of Paper's mother's neck, twisting her around before she fell face-first on to the floor, shaking.

"Noooo!" I hollered bussing my gun. *Boom. Boom. Boom. Boom.* My bullets ripped into the shooter, knocking him backward into the other man that was running toward us.

The other man aimed his gun and shot twice, striking the wall next to the refrigerator.

Boom. Boom. Boom. Boom. "Bitch ass nigga!" *Boom. Boom.* "You shot my mama!" Paper hollered, running at him, letting off shot after shot. *Boom. Boom.* His bullets slammed into the man's torso and stood him up before he fell face-first into the carpet. A pool of blood formed around him. Paper stood over him and let go of two more shots, causing his body to leap into the air.

Fax ran to the front of the house and threw open the front door before flying down the stairs and into his car. Neither me or Paper gave him chase, and I think it was solely because we were taken off guard by the rash of events.

I looked down at Paper's mother. She had her hand around her neck, laying on her back with her leg kicking repeatedly. There was a huge puddle of blood formed around her body. Her eyes were wide open, blinking like crazy. I could hear her choking on her own blood.

Paper ran back into the kitchen and kneeled beside her, pulling her into his arms. "Mama, fight, baby. Please, fight. I'm gon' get you some help, I promise." He pulled out his cellphone and got ready to call the ambulance when she stopped kicking and collapsed in his arms, just as Jamie tried to make his way to his feet.

He got halfway there when I pushed him with brute force back to the floor, stood over him and shot twice. *Boom. Boom.* Both bullets ripped into his forehead before busting out the back of his skull. I stood over him, looking down into his eyes that were wide open yet unseeing. My heart was pounding in my chest. Chills were all over my body. It was like I felt his soul escape from him. I'd taken his life and bits of remorse started to set into me right away.

I felt like the Reaper was standing over my shoulder, smiling down at his corpse. This murder that I'd done all on my own freaked me out just a little bit.

Paper continued to rock back and forth with his mother bleeding out on his arms. He held his fingers up to the holes in her neck, though it did very little to stop the blood from oozing through them. "Why, man? Why did this shit have to happen to her, Rich? She ain't ever hurt nobody," he said with tears running down his cheeks.

After all of the gun firing I knew that the police had to be on their way. Paper's mother lived in a pretty nice neighborhood, so I could only imagine that one of the neighbors had already reported the gunshots, because for that area it wasn't the norm.

"Yo, Paper, we gotta get out of here, man, or we're going to jail. Twelve gotta be on they way here," I said, speaking in terms of the police that were sure to come.

"Why'd you have to shoot at them, Rich? Had you never done that, my mother would still be alive." He whimpered and placed his face into the crux of his mother's neck. The side that wasn't bleeding.

I bugged my eyes out. "What?" I couldn't believe what I was hearing. It sounded like he was trying to blame her murder on me or something. That hurt my heart.

"You heard me, Rich. My mother was all I had, man. She was my everything. My pops locked down, you already know that. The only person I got left out here now is my sister Chasity. Fuck, man." He squeezed her tighter, causing blood to squirt out of her neck holes. The entire kitchen floor looked as if somebody had spilled a bucket of burgundy paint. There was the smell was of burnt flesh.

"Paper, dude shot first. He hit your mother and that's what made me hit his ass up. Him and that other nigga, or else we'd both been dead. I think they are Fax's niggas because he was here too. He ran out the front door after he grabbed all of the money and dope off of the table."

Paper closed his eyes and squeezed them tighter as tears continued to roll down his cheeks. He leaned down and kissed his mother on the forehead, then slowly laid her down on her back before coming to a stand and exhaling loudly. He shook his head, then took off running into his mother's room.

I kneeled and kissed his mother on the forehead and rubbed her soft cheek before closing her eyes with my two fingers. For as long as me and Paper had been friends, she'd been more of a mother to myself than my own biological mother. I loved her and would not stop killing for her until we found Fax and buried his ass in the ground. Whether he'd pulled the trigger or not, he'd still had a hand in it because the dudes were his men, and I was sure that had we not shown up that Fax's plan was to rob and kill Jamie and Paper's mother anyway, though I wasn't entirely sure until much later down the road.

Paper came out of her bedroom with a sheet wrapped up like a big garbage bag. He brushed past me and opened the backdoor. "Come on, bruh, let's get up out of here before the law come. I'll bury my mother later."

As he said those words, I started to hear sirens off in the distance and figured that twelve couldn't have been that far away, so we hit it out the back of her home and made a B-line for Paper's whip, got in and stormed away from the scene with heavy hearts.

Chapter 14

Paper kneeled on the concrete floor of his trap's basement and opened the sheet full of merch that he'd taken from his mother's and Jamie's crib. "I knew that nigga combination the whole time, Rich. My mother told it to me a long time ago, and she said that if anything ever happened to her, that he did it and to clean his safe out. Now look at all this dope this punk had, and this cash." He blinked, and tears rolled down his cheeks.

I could tell that he was still choked up over his mother's murder. After all, it had only been a few hours since it had taken place.

Andrea had been hitting my phone up for the last thirty minutes telling me to watch the news, and that Paper's mother's house was all over it. That she was worried about me and to reach out to her soon. I texted her back that I was okay and that I'd be home in a few hours.

I kneeled beside Paper and put my arm around his shoulder, pulling him to me until his head was against mine. Then, we faced each other and hugged. Both crying tears of pain from the loss of such a great and beautiful woman. She would for surely be missed. "I love you, bruh, and I'm here for you in every way that I can be. I need you to know that."

He continued to cry, nodding, hugging me so hard that it made it difficult for me to breathe. "I know, man. This shit just hurt so bad, Rich. That was my mama." He sobbed into my ear and I couldn't help but to feel some type of way because at my mother's passing I had not broken down like that.

I felt that just maybe Paper may have loved his mother more than I loved my own, and I felt bad about that.

After we got ahold of ourselves, we took inventory of Jamie's merch, and when it was all said and done, Paper had hit him for five kilos of pure cocaine, five kilos of meth and $200,000. He tried to give me half of the money, but I gave back fifteen thousand to put towards giving his mother a proper burial. I took two and a half kilos of coke and two and half kilos of meth, hugged him and promised to get up with him first thing in the afternoon.

When I got back to Andrea's house, she was waiting up for me, sitting at the table in the dining room with a cup of coffee in front of her. I stepped into that room and she jumped up and ran toward me. She stopped when she saw all of the blood that covered my clothes. I dropped the black garbage bag full of money and dope by my Jordan's and shook my head.

Her eyes were as big as saucers. "Rich, what happened? Are you hurt?" She asked rushing to me and checking me for bullet holes, I guessed. After confirming that there weren't any, she took a step back and looked into my eyes with a worried expression.

I lowered my head. "Paper's mother got killed tonight. Some niggas tried to rob her and Jamie, and both of them are dead. It's fucked up." I picked up the bag and started to walk to her room.

Kesha's bedroom door opened, and she came out of it, rubbing her eyes. "Rich, is that you?" She asked, coming into the living room, now blocking my path. Her eyes got big as she saw me covered in the blood.

Andrea put her arm around Kesha's shoulder and ushered her back into her room. "I need to talk to him right now, Kesha. I'll send him in there as soon as I'm done. I promise," Andrea said, closing Kesha's door, then walking behind me. "Baby, we need to get you out of these bloody clothes. It's unsanitary."

I walked into her bedroom, took the bag and poured all of the contents on the top of it. "That's five kilos. I need you to take them and make your mix with them. It's two and half coke, and two and a half meth. I need you to do your thing. It's time that I go hard so we can get the fuck out of this ghetto before something happens to one of y'all, and I'd never be able to live with myself." I blinked, and a tear rolled down my cheek. I started to imagine how Paper's mother looked before we'd left her house. All laid out in a pool of her own blood.

Andrea looked down at the bed with her eyes wide open. "What about the money? What are you going to do with that?"

I pulled my shirt over my head, then did the same with my wife beater because both of them were drenched. I walked into the kitchen, reached under the sink and came up with a Hefty black garbage bag, tossing my dirty clothes inside of it until I was standing there in just my boxers. I walked back into Andrea's room and sat the gun on the dresser, then came out of my boxers as well, just as she stepped into the room after leaving the bathroom. "Take ten of them bands off the bed and put it up for yourself. That money belongs to you, and I don't care what you do with it. Then take another five and pay up some more of the bills so we can go ahead a lil' more. That way, you won't have nothing to worry about for a while."

She nodded and started to count out the $15,000. "Rich, just go and shower. I'll be in there in a second, so I can wash your back. It seems like you've been through a lot, and here you are still trying to take care of other people.

That's cool, but not right now." She stood up and pointed in the direction of the shower.

***

A few minutes later, I entered into the shower stall and allowed for the warm water to rain down on my face. It felt so refreshing though images of the night's events continued to replay themselves over and over in my head. Images so vivid that my heart began to pound in my chest, making me feel as if I were about to pass out. I stuck out an arm and planted it against the wall inside of the shower. Lowering my head, I began to take steady, quick breaths, inhaling and exhaling, while the water beat against my skin.

Andrea pulled back the shower curtain and stepped into the tub with me, getting behind me, where she took a towel and began to lather it with soap before rubbing it all over my muscular back. "You're not alone in all of this, Rich. I'm right here by your side and I ain't ever going nowhere. I love you too much for that, Rich, I swear it." She ran the towel down to my waist, then pulled on my arm until I was facing her.

I allowed for the water to rain down on my back as I looked into her brown eyes. She looked up at me, rubbing my chest with the towel in a circular motion. At that time, I didn't want to think. I didn't want to feel anything emotionally. I needed to escape deep within Andrea. She was the only safe haven that I felt I had this night. So, I pulled her to me and kissed her juicy lips, sucking all over them while my hands cupped her titties and pulled on her thick nipples until she moaned into my mouth lustfully.

"Unnn-a. Rich, do you want me? Is that what you need, lil' daddy, to feel better, huh?" She asked, reaching down and taking ahold of my dick. She stroked it against her belly.

I leaned forward and sucked on her neck while the water popped all over the place. I ran my tongue along the thick vein right on the side of her throat. "Yeah, Andrea. Take me away from this pain, ma. It's getting the best of me right now," I said as Paper's mother flashed into my mind.

I saw an image of her smiling, walking toward me with a nice dinner plate full of food because it was usually how she greeted me whenever Paper and I wound up at his mother's place at night. Her way of showing me love was through her plates of food and hugs. She treated me as if I was her son.

Andrea pushed me back a lil' bit, then sank to her knees, stroking my pipe before taking it and sucking it into her mouth. I watched her head go back and forth quickly. The heat from her mouth was driving me insane. I squeezed my eyes tighter and allowed myself to drift off into the land of Andrea. It felt so good. I grabbed a handful of her hair and guided her movements, even though I didn't have to because she was all pro in my book.

She licked all around the head then popped me out of her mouth. She stood up, looking me in the eyes before bending over and spreading her legs. "Fuck me, Rich. Take all of your pain out on this bald pussy. Look at it, baby." She reached under herself and rubbed all over her naked mound before prying the lips apart and showing me her pink hole. "You see that, lil' daddy? Does that make you happy?" She slid a finger into herself and ran it in and out for a moment, then pulled it out and smacked herself on the ass, causing water to splash.

My dick was throbbing so much that it hurt. I took my pipe and ran it up and down her sex lips, moving them apart by the use of my head before slowly easing into her furnace.

Her lips opened up, accepting my invasion before she slammed backward and swallowed him whole. "Ahh!" she screamed, then placed both of her hands on the wall.

I took her hips and pushed her forward, only to yank her back to me again and again, while she yelped and moaned at the top of her lungs. The feel of her big booty bouncing into me drove me crazy. Her pussy felt like a slice of paradise. I watched her ass ripple with each assault, along with the jiggle of her titties. Our skins slapping together sounded like handclaps. *Clap, clap, clap, clap, clap, clap, clap.* My dick drove deep into her womb, hitting a soft bottom.

"Un, un, un, un, Rich, yes, daddy, yes, lil' daddy. Un, fuck me. Take it out, un, on, me, Rich, harder, please!" She moaned, crashing back into me.

I closed my eyes and put one of my feet up on the rim of the tub, pulling her back into me and fucking her as hard as I could. Her pussy sucked at my pole like a hungry mouth, sending tingles throughout my body. Because Andrea was so strapped, her ass couldn't stop shaking as I crashed into her, digging deep into her belly. "Yeah, Andrea. Take. This. Dick. Baby. Oooh, yeah!"

"Rich, Rich, Rich, uhh-a, Rich, you fucking me so hard. You fucking me so hard, Rich! I'm cumming! Uhhh-a!" She screamed, crashing back into me harder and harder.

I had ahold of her hips, killing that shit with my eyes wide open, watching her flesh jiggle and loving the way it looked for my dick to drive in and out of her pussy, over and over again. When she reached behind herself and held her ass cheeks open, that's when I couldn't hold back anymore. Her womb was already sucking at me and vibrating.

The sight of her asshole was just too much. I started to cum deep within her belly. "Arrrgh!" I growled through clenched teeth, ramming into her harder and harder, trying to release all of my pains into her womb. I felt my seed shooting out of me and into her, and it made me weak.

She bit into her lower lip and moaned at the top of her lungs, "My ass, Rich. Save some for my ass, daddy, please. I need it so bad, uhhhh-a! Shit!" She crashed into me three hard times, milking me, then leaned all the way forward so that my dick slipped out of her box. She turned around and sucked me until I was just as hard as before, bent back over and spread her ass cheeks. "Now, there, daddy. Fuck me right there. Come on." She growled, then bent herself at an awkward angle so she could see me sliding into her backdoor.

I rubbed all around inside of her kitty lips, getting my fingers slippery wet, then placed it on to her asshole before taking my head and slipping into her, while she continued to hold her cheeks wide open. They were so soft and meaty. Andrea was so thick. She had one of those down south bodies that drove men like me crazy. I couldn't get enough of it as I stuffed her over and over.

"Huh, huh, huh, huh, huh, yes, Rich. Oooo-a, fuck my ass, baby. Umm-a, yes, daddy. Ooo-a, it hurt so good-a!" She hollered.

I grabbed her hair and pulled her head backward. It forced her to arch her back as she bounced into me. Her pussy would stick to my nuts before unsticking. All of it was driving me out of my mind as I got to fucking her with everything that I had. *Bam, bam, bam, bam, bam, bam, bam, bam!*

"Uhhhh! I'm cumming again, Rich! Oooh, shit I'm cumming!" She threw her head back and screamed while I kept on pounding that fat ass out.

I was on the verge of cumming along with her. I felt it building deep within my balls, when suddenly there was a loud banging on the door.

"Rich! Andrea! Y'all making too much noise in there! Shut up!" Kesha hollered.

I tried to block her voice out of my head as I continued to pound into Andrea harder and harder. I needed to release myself one more time into her, and I was so close. I sped up the pace. *Bam, bam, bam, bam, bam, bam.* "Arrggh!"

Andrea lowered her head and shook it, bouncing back into me just as hard as I was pounding into her. "Okay, Kesha! Go lay down. Go lay down! Please!" She begged.

I yanked Andrea's head backward by her hair, stood on my tippy toes and came deep within her ass, jerking along the way. "Uhh, uh, uh. This shit so good." I whispered, still letting my seed fly. I leaned over her back with my dick still deep within her and kissed her lips before tonguing her down.

Seconds later, Kesha beat back on the door. "I hope y'all know that Keyonna ain't in her room."

I frowned, slid out of Andrea, and finished my shower before getting out and wrapping a towel around me. Only then did I answer the door.

Kesha was standing right outside of it with her arms crossed. "Well, I see y'all ain't shy to let the whole world know that y'all getting down together." She blew air through her teeth and shook her head in disappointment.

I wasn't trying to get into that at that moment, though I knew that I would have too soon because me and Andrea had never taken the time out to explain to my sister what it was that she and I had going on. To be honest, I don't think we thoroughly knew. "Kesha, how long has Keyonna been gone, huh?"

Kesha tried to look over my shoulder. I looked back and saw that Andrea was sitting on the edge of the tub, looking as if she was exhausted. "She been gone for two days now. I thought she came home last night, but I guess she didn't. She missing a lot of clothes, too." She turned her back on me and walked off.

I hurried into Andrea's room and got dressed. Andrea walked into the room yawning with her hands over her head. She'd chosen to put on one of my white t-shirts that did little to mask her nipple imprints.

I couldn't believe how fine she was, but I had to snap out of it. "Andrea, why you ain't tell me that my sister been missing from the crib like that?" I asked, grabbing my phone off of the dresser and calling Keyonna's line.

I felt sick to my stomach that I had missed something so important. I prayed that she wasn't running behind Kendell, even though I knew the chances of her not were slim to none.

Andrea shrugged. "All that girl want to do is argue these days. I ain't got no time for that, Rich. We trying to accomplish too much, and you can't keep babying her. She's a grown woman and she gon' keep on doing whatever she wants to. That's just how it is." She started to rake up the money after taking the kilos and setting them on top of the dresser beside my pistol that I had yet to get rid of.

I shook my head and was about to tear into her ass verbally when Keyonna picked up on the other end. "What's up, Rich?" She asked dryly.

I scrunched my face, feeling my anger getting the better of me. I tried my best to calm down. I didn't want her to detect that I was furious with her. "Where are you, Keyonna? Why haven' you been home in a couple days?" I asked as smoothly as possible.

She exhaled loudly. "Because I ain't coming back there. That's why."

I felt like I had been punched in the gut by a heavy-weight boxer. "What you mean you ain't coming back here? When did you make that decision?" I asked, sitting on the bed because my knees got weak real fast.

"Look, Rich, I'm a grown woman and I can make my own decisions. I don't want to live there no more. I'm tired of arguing with Andrea, I'm tired of not having my privacy, and most of all I'm tired of you telling me what to do. I'm a woman now, and I can make my own way just fine."

I felt like I wanted to throw up. There was no way that I could lose my little sister. I loved her with all of my heart and I knew that it had to be Ken and his son getting into her head because I had never heard her talk to me the way that she was.

Sweat appeared on my brow as I tried to remain calm. "Keyonna, can we just talk about this over lunch or something? I mean, we have to come up with a plan to make sure that you're good for the long haul. I can't have you out there in those streets struggling to get by. You're my baby sister, and I love you, ma. So at least grant me that." I stood up, pacing with my phone pressed to my ear.

Keyonna sucked her teeth loudly. "I'm good. My man will take care of me from here on out. I don't need nobody's help other than his. I'm sorry if you're mad at mem Rich, but I just need to be free. I love Kendell, and I can't be away from him. I have to prove to him that I am worthy of his love, and I will. Take care of yourself and I'll see you around." She disconnected the call.

I slumped to the floor with my heart split in two.

***

It took me two whole days to gather myself, and in that timespan Keyonna did not call or text anybody in the house. I was sure that Kendell had gotten into her head, and it had me so mentally discombobulated that I couldn't think straight. Once again, I had murder on my mind. I had to find out where Ken and Kendell lived so I could get my sister back while making them pay for their sins.

Chapter 15

I had my arm around Paper's shoulder as we watched his mother's casket being lowered into the ground, and a sudden state of déjà vu came over me. It had been a little more than a year since I'd watched my own mother's coffin being lowered into the ground, and all at once the emotions from that day came back to me. I hugged my right-hand man and patted him on the back. "She in a better place now, man. We gotta keep her memory alive and go at that nigga Fax for making this happen. I'm riding with you until the end. You got my blood on that."

Paper nodded and exhaled loudly as the thunder roared in the sky before the rain started. He took one last look down into the hole and shook his head. "It's good, bruh. We gon' get him when the time is right. But first, let's get rich like we're supposed to be." He hugged me again before jogging to his car.

I looked into his mother's grave and said a silent prayer in my head, asking the Lord to accept Paper's mother into heaven, and for her to forgive us for the things that she was about to witness us do from up above.

I looked out at the crowded service as the rain began to pour and shook my head. I started to have premonitions. For some reason I felt that I wouldn't be alive for that much longer. I didn't know why I was feeling that way, but I was. I got to thinking about my sisters and Andrea. Who would take care of them when I was gone? Who would be their protector? I didn't know and that scared me. I had to make sure that by the time God took me off of this earth that my people were well off and, in a position, to fend for themselves, and I also needed to track Keyonna down, so I could talk some sense into her. I missed her so much, and every day without her was killing me softly.

Aaliyah contacted me the night of Paper's mother's funeral and told me to meet her out at the motel because she had some important news for me and she needed me there right away.

When I arrived, she opened the door and ran into my arms, wrapping them around my neck. "I missed you so much, Rich. I been sick without you." She stepped onto her tippy toes and kissed my lips, rubbing the side of my face with her eyes closed.

I held her close to me. Her feminine scent wafted up my nose, intoxicating me as it always had. I hugged her then released my hold. "That bitch nigga's son got my sister, and now she done ran away from home, saying she ain't ever coming back," I said, feeling my anger rise.

Aaliyah bucked her eyes and shook her head. "That's not good, Rich. Kendell is just like his father. In fact, Ken uses him to go out and recruit younger girls for him. That boy does everything just to get his father's approval. It's almost sickening." She walked over to me and rubbed my chest. "What are you going to do, baby?" She looked up at me with her pretty eyes and gorgeous face, concerned.

I shook my head. "I don't know yet. What is the reason you needed me over here so badly?"

She bit into her bottom lip, then ran her fingers through her hair, turning her back on me. "Well, the news is not so great now considering this turn of events, but tomorrow has to be the day you hit this lick. You'll be able to walk away with everything that he has. I'm talking at least a million dollars' worth of product, and I don't even know how much cash, but it's going to be sweet." She turned around and looked into my eyes. "That is if you're still down to go through with this."

I sat on the bed and ran my hands over my face. The whole thing with Keyonna was throwing me off so bad that I felt like I was about to have a nervous breakdown. I couldn't understand why my little sister would turn on the family like that when I've always made it was my business to spoil her and keep her first alongside Kesha. I tried to mentally go through the chapters of my mind to see where I had gone wrong.

Aaliyah came over and kneeled at my feet, placing both of her small hands on my knees. "Rich, say something. I'm so worried about you right now."

I took my hands away and looked down at her. "Man, this shit with my sister is fucking me up because everything I do out in these streets, I do for them first and foremost. I thought that I've always given her everything that she needed, when it turns out that she was looking for an exit the entire time, and I don't know how to process that in my heart. I'm sick, and it's just getting the better of me because I have failed as a brother."

Aaliyah shook her head. "Never, baby. What you have to realize is that Ken and Kendell are pimps. They are wordsmiths and they know how to appeal to the emptiness in a girl. Your sister has probably been through a lot, just like you have, and Kendell knows that. It's his job to step in and make her to feel as if he can heal her. That he's all she'll need from here on out, and that losing him would be the worst pain that she has ever felt in her entire life. Once he gets her to believe that, she's in trouble, and I can bet you my last dollar that it's the angle he worked on her. Which is why when Ken goes, he should also." She shook her head. "Those two have done some things to me that I never want to speak of. I hate them both so much that I can't even tell you how much." She looked off into space for a long time, then shook herself out of the trance. "I know where they are, baby, and we can get them. All you have to say is when?" She took my hand and placed it so that I was cuffing the side of her small, oval shaped face.

For some reason, just feeling her skin against my own helped me to feel a little bit better. I pulled her up and wrapped my arms around her, kissing her forehead and then her lips. "We gon' handle this business with this white dude first. Get this bread and this dope before I handle Ken and his punk ass son. I think that's the only way my sister gon' forget about this nigga is if I take him out the game. I know that he all in her head and she's vulnerable. We've been through a lot, and she'd never had nobody feeding her mental the way that they're probably doing every single day. I wish I would have done a better job, honestly."

Aaliyah rubbed my chest. "I'm sure that you did the best you could, considering the circumstances." She kissed my lips again. "Alright then, I'll spend a night with him tonight, and get everything in order so you can hit him up the first thing in the morning. That way we can put all of this shit behind us, and I can watch you knock off Ken and Kendell's punk assed. It'll be my joy." She smiled and hugged me tightly.

I didn't know if I was going to let her watch me do nothing. We had never agreed to nothing like that, but I didn't feel like arguing at that time. All I wanted to do was hold her until my mind cleared. Then, we sat down, and she gave me the ins and outs of the lick.

***

The next morning, after me and Paper grabbed everything that we'd need in order to pull of this caper, we found ourselves parked two blocks over from the Vick's crib, smoking a blunt and trying to get ourselves mentally prepared to make it happen.

Paper put fire to the end of the Dutch and inhaled deeply. Then, he blew the smoke back out. "Bruh, if this lick is as one hunnit as ol' girl saying it is, then we about to get our money all the way up. I got this hype that got these properties all around Milwaukee. We can flood this bitch and really get paid. I got about twenty of them young niggas that a work up under us. You know, lil' hungry goons whose families out here starving. We gon' put them down and spread them out and capitalize off of the game. That way we'll be rich in no time, you feel me?" He took three more deep pulls and passed me the blunt as my phone vibrated with a text from Aaliyah, telling me that everything was good.

I took four quick pulls off of the blunt and inhaled them deeply before handing the blunt back to Paper and blowing the smoke to the ceiling. "Bruh, that sound like a plan. Shorty seem one hunnit to me, and you know I got trust issues. I think she tellin' the truth, and if she ain't, then we 'bout to find out because she just texted me, telling me that the garage is open, so let's move."

I loaded all of my things up on me and slid my white ski mask over my face, waited until Paper stubbed out the blunt before he did the same thing, then we were out of the car and sprinting down the alley that lead up to the Vick's block. Coming to the gate, we jumped it and ended up in his big backyard, just as the sun started to peak through the clouds.

The air felt moist and I could tell that it was setting up to be an extremely humid day. I took a deep breath as we came to the side of his garage, right next to a huge green bush that made me, and Paper kneel and walk around before we were in his drive way. Then, we dashed inside of the garage that had two Jaguars parked inside— one all red and the other all black. Both looked as if they were newly released off of the showroom floor.

The first thing I thought was that this nigga had money, and I couldn't wait to get my hands on it along with his dope.

Paper came and kneeled beside me. "Them muhfuckas fresh right there, bruh. Damn, I wish we could hit his bitch ass for them. Could you imagine?" He shook his head and pulled his pistol out of his waistband, cocking it back.

I did the same thing before creeping toward the garage door that led into the house. Paper stayed crouched down as I reached and slowly turned the knob, pushing the door inward just a little bit so I could peer inside. The first thing I saw was a German Sheppard with its face inside of a doggy bowl. It was all brown and looked full grown.

As the door creaked open, the dog picked up its head and looked in my direction before growling and slowly walking over to where I was. As soon as it got there, I closed the door a little to see what it would do. It came over and sniffed along the crack, whining, then raised its paw and scratched at the door before turning around and walking further into the house where I watched him disappear around the corner. I can't lie and say that didn't get me worried because, according to Aaliyah, she was going to be sexing the Vick upstairs in his master bedroom. While she was doing so, we were to come in and break them up and force the man to take us to the merch, which

172

for us wouldn't have been a problem. Now, there was this dog. I didn't know if he was vicious or just a mutt, and that was a cause for concern.

Paper climbed the short steps until he was behind me and kneeled back down. "What's good, bruh? Why we ain't in this bitch yet?" He asked, moving uncomfortably. For as long as I'd known the homey he'd always said something about having bad knees, so I could tell that they were bothering him.

"It's a dog in there," I whispered, opening the door a little wider. "I don't know if that muhfucka a killa or not. What if we gotta murk it?" I asked, opening the door all the way.

Paper sucked his teeth. "Then that's just what we gotta do. Fuck that dog. Let's go and get this money, nigga." He slapped me on the back.

A minute later we were on our way up the stairs, and still there was no sign of the animal, but trust me I was on high alert. Every sound that I heard caused my heart to pound harder in my chest. By this point I was hoping that the dog jumped out, so we could handle him and get it over with. I hated surprises.

Me and Paper made our way down the long, white carpeted hallway. The Vick had paintings all along his walls, and the carpet was so thick that my shoes sank into it. It felt like I was walking on a cloud, or at least how I'd imagine walking on a cloud to feel.

Paper kept close behind me with his gun out, looking in all directions, and so did I. I couldn't believe that this Vick was supposed to have all of this dope and money inside of this house, and yet there was no security. It sent red flags up in my mind and made me a bit more nervous. I cocked the hammer on my Glock and took another deep breath as we got closer and closer to the master bedroom door at the end of the hallway.

I was about ten feet away when I heard the distinct sounds of passionate love making and the squeaking of bedsprings.

Paper stepped forward and placed his ear on the door, then looked back to me and nodded. "Let's go, bruh. Handle this business and we gon' be rich men. You ready?" He whispered so low that I could barely hear him.

I nodded, took a step back, raised my foot and kicked the door with all of my might. *Whoom!* The door flew inward and nearly came off the hinges. Then, Paper ran past me with his gun out. There was a loud scream from inside as I gathered myself.

"Everybody get the fuck down. This the one and only time I'mma say it!" Paper hollered, rushing toward the bed.

I ran in right behind him, ready to go into action until I looked out at the couple and was able to identify the man. My heart dropped into my stomach and I felt like I could no longer breathe as I watched Paper grab him by the neck before slapping him across the face with his pistol, causing his blood to skeet across the headboard. He flew backward as Paper grabbed him again and jammed his pistol to his forehead, cocking the hammer.

Aaliyah jumped out of the bed and slid her hand underneath it, coming up with a key. "Y'all gotta kill him or we all fucked. It ain't gon' matter because I got the key to his safe, so we good." She ran around to me and got ready to kiss me on the cheek as I stood frozen in place, unable to move by the sights of him.

Paper grabbed a big pillow and placed it over his face, putting the barrel of his gun against it, I imagined ready to blow his brains all over the mattress while he laid there, barely moving, weak from the attack. "Say yo' prayers, white man."

I snapped out of my zone and ran toward the bed with haste. "Bruh, wait, don't kill 'em! That's my father!"

To Be Continued...
Traphouse King 2
Coming Soon

Submission Guideline.

Submit the first three chapters of your completed manuscript to ldpsubmissions@gmail.com, subject line: Your book's title. The manuscript must be in a .doc file and sent as an attachment. Document should be in Times New Roman, double spaced and in size 12 font. Also, provide your synopsis and full contact information. If sending multiple submissions, they must each be in a separate email.

Have a story but no way to send it electronically? You can still submit to LDP/Ca$h Presents. Send in the first three chapters, written or typed, of your completed manuscript to:

LDP: Submissions Dept
Po Box 870494
Mesquite, Tx 75187

DO NOT send original manuscript. Must be a duplicate.

Provide your synopsis and a cover letter containing your full contact information.

Thanks for considering LDP and Ca$h Presents.

A DRUG KING AND HIS DIAMOND **II**
By **Nicole Goosby**
SHE FELL IN LOVE WITH A REAL ONE
By **Tamara Butler**

Available Now
RESTRAINING ORDER **I & II**
By **CA$H & Coffee**
LOVE KNOWS NO BOUNDARIES **I II & III**
By **Coffee**
RAISED AS A GOON I, II, III & IV
BRED BY THE SLUMS I, II, III
BLAST FOR ME
By **Ghost**
LAY IT DOWN **I & II**
LAST OF A DYING BREED
BLOOD STAINS OF A SHOTTA I & II
By **Jamaica**
LOYAL TO THE GAME
LOYAL TO THE GAME II
LOYAL TO THE GAME III
By **TJ & Jelissa**
BLOODY COMMAS I & II
SKI MASK CARTEL
By **T.J. Edwards**
IF LOVING HIM IS WRONG…I & II
By **Jelissa**
WHEN THE STREETS CLAP BACK I & II
By **Jibril Williams**
A DISTINGUISHED THUG STOLE MY HEART I & II
By **Meesha**
PUSH IT TO THE LIMIT
By **Bre' Hayes**
BLOOD OF A BOSS **I, II, III & IV**
By **Askari**
THE STREETS BLEED MURDER **I, II & III**
THE HEART OF A GANGSTA I II& III
By **Jerry Jackson**
CUM FOR ME
CUM FOR ME 2

CUM FOR ME 3
An **LDP Erotica Collaboration**
BRIDE OF A HUSTLA **I & II**
THE FETTI GIRLS **I, II& III**
By **Destiny Skai**
WHEN A GOOD GIRL GOES BAD
By **Adrienne**
A GANGSTER'S REVENGE **I II III & IV**
THE BOSS MAN'S DAUGHTERS
THE BOSS MAN'S DAUGHTERS II
THE BOSSMAN'S DAUGHTERS III
THE BOSSMAN'S DAUGHTERS IV
A SAVAGE LOVE **I & II**
BAE BELONGS TO ME
A HUSTLER'S DECEIT I, II
By **Aryanna**
A KINGPIN'S AMBITON
A KINGPIN'S AMBITION **II**
I MURDER FOR THE DOUGH
By **Ambitious**
TRUE SAVAGE
TRUE SAVAGE II
TRUE SAVAGE **III**
By **Chris Green**
A DOPEBOY'S PRAYER
By **Eddie "Wolf" Lee**
THE KING CARTEL **I, II & III**
By **Frank Gresham**
THESE NIGGAS AIN'T LOYAL **I, II & III**
By **Nikki Tee**
GANGSTA SHYT **I II &III**
By **CATO**
THE ULTIMATE BETRAYAL
By **Phoenix**
BOSS'N UP **I , II & III**
By **Royal Nicole**
I LOVE YOU TO DEATH
By **Destiny J**
I RIDE FOR MY HITTA
I STILL RIDE FOR MY HITTA

By **Misty Holt**
LOVE & CHASIN' PAPER
By **Qay Crockett**
TO DIE IN VAIN
By **ASAD**
BROOKLYN HUSTLAZ
By **Boogsy Morina**
BROOKLYN ON LOCK I & II
By **Sonovia**
GANGSTA CITY
By **Teddy Duke**
A DRUG KING AND HIS DIAMOND
A DOPEMAN'S RICHES
By Nicole Goosby
TRAPHOUSE KING
By **Hood Rich**

BOOKS BY LDP'S CEO, CA$H

TRUST IN NO MAN
TRUST IN NO MAN 2
TRUST IN NO MAN 3
BONDED BY BLOOD
SHORTY GOT A THUG
THUGS CRY
THUGS CRY 2
THUGS CRY 3
TRUST NO BITCH
TRUST NO BITCH 2
TRUST NO BITCH 3
TIL MY CASKET DROPS
RESTRAINING ORDER
RESTRAINING ORDER 2
IN LOVE WITH A CONVICT

Coming Soon
BONDED BY BLOOD 2
BOW DOWN TO MY GANGSTA

HOOD RICH